MW00717087

"You'd better get
It's getting close to five and Aunt Cammie
always has the meal ready on time."

Maggie almost jumped out of her new boots. She twisted around and saw Drake. "I didn't see you behind me."

"You should be more alert. I could have been a bear," he growled as he carried the crate of supplies past her.

"You are a bear, Mr. Strong," Maggie spoke loud and clear as she placed her hands on her hips.

Drake immediately stopped and dropped the crate to the ground. He stood tall and held his back rigid to her for a moment. When he turned to face her, he had a smile on his lips that didn't quite reach his eyes. He slowly stepped toward her, and she had to make a conscious effort not to retreat.

"I should warn you, Maggie," he stepped within the realm of her personal space before continuing. "As your host, I can make your stay here pleasurable, or I can make it a living nightmare. Which do you prefer?"

Maggie closed the gaping hole in her mouth to speak. "P-probably the former, Mr. Strong. I mean Drake. I apologize. My runaway mouth has gotten me into trouble more than once."

His gaze lowered to her lips. "I don't doubt that for a minute." As his eyes traveled back to hers, they turned a shade darker.

She moistened her dry lips. He watched.

She fought hard to find her voice. "I've been a bit on edge, lately. With all that's been happening..." Her voice trailed off. "Maybe we can start over."

"You're mistaken. There is no *we*." He turned and picked up the crate, walking away without a backward glance.

Kudos for Wendy Davy

"A heart-warming story of faith, love and second chances. Ms. Davy weaves a story that touches hearts and reaffirms the strength of the human spirit."

~*Anne Seymour*, editor, The Wild Rose Press

A MATTER OF TRUST, also by Wendy Davy, has recently been published by The Wild Rose Press.

Drake's Retreat

by

Wendy Davy

For: Aunt Judy
Enjoy!
Wendy Davy

Drake's Retreat

COPYRIGHT © 2008 by Wendy J. Davy

Cover Art by *Kim Mendoza*

The Wild Rose Press
PO Box 706
Adams Basin, NY 14410-0706
Visit us at www.thewildrosepress.com

Publishing History
First White Rose Edition, 2008
Print ISBN 1-60154-328-X

Published in the United States of America

Dedication

For Brian, Samantha, Travis and Jessica
Special thanks to:
Aunt Teresa for her helpful advice,
Aunt Judy for her encouragement and inspiration,
Debbie and Kathy, for the kind of friendship that
lasts forever.

"Trust in the Lord with all your heart, And lean not on your own understanding; In all your ways acknowledge Him, And He shall direct your paths." Proverbs 3:5-6

Chapter One

"I don't have a husband," Maggie Reynolds' statement caught everyone's attention. All chatter stopped and she cast a glance at the curious faces watching her. She felt heat climb up her cheeks and it had nothing to do with the unusually warm, early September day. She ignored the other resort guests and kept her attention on the man standing in front of her.

The broad shouldered lumberjack of a man stared at her in silence. He ran his deep blue eyes over her, as if he searched for what was wrong with her.

Maggie added, "The two weeks at your resort are paid for. What does it matter anyway?"

"This is a couples retreat. Specifically designed for couples. I assure you, Miss Reynolds, it does matter."

Maggie's heart tripped a beat. He wouldn't really turn her away, would he? She pasted a smile on her face to hide her growing anxiety. "I won't be a bother to anyone. I'll keep to myself and..."

"Keeping to yourself is precisely the problem, ma'am. My cabins are in a very remote area of the Sierra Nevada Mountains. Going off on your own is strictly prohibited. I lead the group excursions, but any hiking or exploring aside from that must be with a partner."

She searched for a concrete reason he couldn't turn her away. She came up blank as she met his steely glare. Maggie squared her shoulders. "Look, Mr.?"

"Mr. Drake Strong."

Maggie studied the owner of the resort, searching for a glimpse of compassion. His too long, dark hair did nothing to hide the irritation that crossed his rugged features. He stood with his muscled arms crossed and his booted feet wide apart. She saw no more compassion in him than she did in the bark on the tree rooted behind him.

"Mr. Strong, I won't be any trouble. I need to be here," she said trying to keep the desperation out of her voice.

The sturdy owner swept his eyes over her. "Are you sure you wouldn't be more comfortable in a spa resort setting. There's a nice one not too far away from here. I'm willing to give you a full refund."

Maggie tilted her head and lifted her chin a notch. "Don't presume to know me Mr. Strong. I'm tougher than I look. I can handle a little bit of wilderness," she spoke in a smooth voice, trying to hide her uncertainty.

Bold laughter erupted from his throat. "A little bit of wilderness? Lady, you have no idea." He captured her hand in his and lifted it to inspect her fingernails. "These manicured nails wouldn't last a day."

Maggie yanked her hand out of his rough, warm grasp. "You're mistaking me for someone who would care. I'm not leaving." Maggie crossed her arms and tapped her right foot. She tried to ignore the lingering warmth where he had briefly touched her.

"Suit yourself. But you have to follow the rules. No one goes off alone. No hiking, caving or any kind of exploring by yourself. Not anywhere. If you want to be a tag along…" his voice trailed off as he gave an exasperated shrug.

She took his answer as affirmative and she nodded. "Fine." Maggie plopped herself on one of the log benches next to the other guests waiting to be transported to the remote cabins and shoved her hair back from her face. She avoided eye contact with him as she flipped opened the brochure for Drake's Retreat, but she could feel his penetrating eyes remaining focused on her. She tried to look at ease, but her heart still beat at a frantic pace. Would he change his mind and send her away?

Finally, she saw Mr. Strong turn and walk away at a leisurely pace. She let out a pent up breath and her shoulders sagged in relief. She did it. Now, she would have a chance to start picking up the pieces of her shattered life and try to figure out how to paste them back together again.

Her eyes scanned the brochure of the resort where she had won the right to spend the next two weeks. She read the first line three times before giving up. Her mind couldn't focus enough to allow the words to make sense.

A light tap on her shoulder from behind made Maggie jump. She turned to find the youngest member of the group smiling at her.

The doe-eyed woman leaned forward and whispered, "You've got grit to stand up to such an intimidating man." Her conspiratorial smile widened. "He's cute though, don't you think?"

Maggie liked the young brunette immediately. She remembered a time long ago when she had been as carefree as the young woman looked.

"I'm Maggie Reynolds." She introduced herself.

"Oh, my. Now I've forgotten my manners. I'm Cyndi Marcus. I'm here on my honeymoon. Why'd he ask where your husband is? Are you supposed to be married?" she asked without reserve.

"It's a long story." Maggie shrugged.

"Well, whatever happened, remember there's a reason for everything. Maybe you'll be better off

anyhow. Look at Mr. Hunk. He's watching you."
Cyndi Marcus looked past Maggie's shoulder.

Maggie's gut reaction almost made her turn around and look, but she caught herself just in time and continued to look at Cyndi. "Mr. Strong doesn't like me. Even if he did, I'm not interested."

"Why on earth not?" Cyndi gave her an incredulous, you're out of your mind stare.

"The last thing I need right now is a man."

"Even if he's hot?"

"Aren't you supposed to be a newlywed?" Maggie accused.

"I am, honey," Cyndi answered dreamy-eyed while resting her chin on the palm of her hand. "But I can still recognize eye-candy when I see it."

Maggie laughed, which helped to release some of the tension that had built up in the last few weeks.

Cyndi added, "You know. I heard that Mr. Strong designed the cabins himself, and built them with his own two hands. Could be just a rumor, but by looking at him? I'd believe it."

Maggie cast a quick glance over her shoulder at him and noticed his broad shoulders bunch as he hauled luggage to a long, narrow dock jutting out from the shoreline. Maggie looked past him to the lake that lay beyond and wondered why he was moving the guest's luggage onto the dock.

She turned back to Cyndi and said, "The brochure says the rockers on the porches are handmade. Maybe he carved them out of a tree." Maggie intended her comment as a joke, but just from the looks of him, she imagined him capable of a lot of things.

Cyndi giggled again. "There is some interest in your eyes. I can see it."

"No. If you knew what I've been through recently, you wouldn't say that."

A tall, lanky young man walked over and straddled the bench next to Cyndi and wrapped his affectionate arms around her. A fuzzy growth of beard lined his angled jaw and his long hair hung down his back in a ponytail. He directed his warm expression to his new wife.

Cyndi introduced them. "Dillon, this is Maggie." She leaned in, and snuggled with her husband.

He took a brief look at Maggie and nodded. "Nice to meet you," he said with sincerity before he turned his attention straight back to Cyndi.

"You too."

Cyndi immediately turned her full attention to her new groom as if Maggie had ceased to exist. Maggie felt more amused than awkward and turned around with a hint of a smile and a shake of her head. A slight wisp of a breeze carried a wavy strand of hair across her eyes and she absently reached up to tuck it behind her ear.

Her brief smile faded as thoughts of Nathan invaded her. He had never liked to show affection in public, or anywhere else for that matter. A fresh stab of pain washed through her. What would it be like to be head over heels in love like Cyndi and Dillon? Maggie chewed on her bottom lip. She didn't know the answer, and yet she was supposed to have gotten married yesterday.

Determined to put Nathan out of her thoughts, she opened up the resort's brochure again and reviewed the pages. Maggie knew from a brief look at the information once before that Drake Strong owned a large portion of wilderness which backed up to the Sierra Nevada National Forest. The pictures showed a quaint, yet rustic setting on a clear blue lake that drew her into daydreams of rest and tranquility.

Maggie flipped the brochure to the back and her breath caught in her throat. Uh-Oh. A list of must have equipment printed in bold-red lined the page. How could she have missed it before? She didn't have one thing on the list. No mosquito repellant, hiking boots, long underwear or gloves. Even a handheld GPS system made the list. Like she would know how to use one of those gadgets anyway. She suddenly felt ill-prepared as she swatted at a mosquito. Too late, it had bitten her. She felt the annoying itch already. *Great.*

Maggie sneaked a peek at the other guest's feet. She felt even more unprepared when she discovered they all wore hiking boots. Cyndi and her new husband had them on, a couple in their early fifties had them on. Even the last couple in the group had them on. They looked too old to hike, but they still had them on.

She felt a tinge of embarrassment and wished she had more time to prepare for this trip as she looked down at her meek tennis shoes. Were they adequate for the rough terrain? As she studied the soles looking for answers, a tall shadow closed in over her.

Maggie's eyes slowly trailed up to a pair of well-worn boots resting in front of her. Then her eyes traveled further up to a pair of well-worn jeans. Then they finally found the well-worn eyes of Drake Strong. His blue eyes reminded her of the deep sea, turbulent and unforgiving. Maggie guessed him to be in his early thirties, but his eyes held the secrets of a much more experienced man.

"Wondering if those shoes are adequate?" He directed his low voice to her alone.

How did he read her mind? Her annoyance level hitched up a notch as she asked, "Are they?"

"For around camp they are, but not for hiking or caving. Since you'll be going to the resort without a partner, you won't be allowed to remain behind if everyone else chooses to go on an excursion. So, I would suggest you buy some new hiking boots at Jenkins Store. He'll have what you need." He pointed to one of the many quaint village stores that lined the large lake at the check-in center.

"I know I'm coming on this retreat alone and so does everyone else." Maggie looked around at the other guests who pretended to mind their own business. "So, you don't have to keep reminding me. I'll get some boots. I like to hike anyway."

He gave her another quick perusal and sent her a doubtful look before he turned on his heel and strode to the front of the group.

Maggie wanted to stick her tongue out at him but decided she better not. She'd behave for now and save her opinions for later. He still might refuse to let her come if she deliberately provoked him.

"Good afternoon and welcome everyone. I'm Drake Strong, owner and operator of Drake's Retreat. Is everyone ready for an adventure?" He asked and smiled when the guests seemed eager to hear more. Maggie sucked in a breath when she saw his lips turn upward. Drake Strong was a handsome man even with a scowl on his face, but when he smiled, he transformed into nothing short of gorgeous. She couldn't blame Cyndi for noticing. Maggie tore her eyes off the charming dimple on his cheek and concentrated on his next words.

"We'll have a brief introduction then go over some rules."

Maggie watched as each of the guests introduced themselves. All together, seven guests waited on the benches to go to Drake Strong's all inclusive resort. The first couple to speak up, Beverly and Stephen Riley, looked to be in their early fifties. Beverly wore tailored slacks and a matching cardigan with layers of jewelry. She sat with a stiff back and held her head high as she spoke her name in a rigid monotone.

Maggie looked at Beverly's husband, Stephen, as he stood tall, ran a hand over his thick, gel-coated hair and adjusted his neck tie. He gave his name to the group then bent slightly at the waist.

"Oh, sit down. You don't need to impress anyone

here," his wife snapped.

"Speak for yourself, Bev," Stephen said as he turned to Maggie and winked, earning his wife's elbow in his gut. Maggie quickly averted her eyes as she felt a tinge of unease.

The older couple, Annie and Larry Remmings, sat cuddled close to each other with bright smiles on their aging faces. Annie announced the fact that they were also newlyweds. Cyndi and Dillon Marcus introduced themselves next. They untangled themselves from each other long enough to tell their names.

Maggie tried to commit each of the names to memory. If she didn't make a conscience effort to try to remember names, she'd forget as soon as the person spoke them.

She heard Drake Strong prompt, "Miss Reynolds. Care to introduce yourself?"

Great. Now that she had been interrupted, she would forget their names and embarrass herself later. Mr. Strong began to progress from mildly annoying to downright irritating. She drew her gaze from the resort owner and saw each of the guests staring at her expectantly.

"Oh, yes. I'm Maggie Reynolds." She looked back at Drake Strong and added, "The crazy woman who dares to go on a couples retreat without a husband." Her remark earned giggles from behind her.

Cyndi piped up, "Seems we have a dare-devil in our midst."

Laughter erupted from the guests, and Maggie couldn't help but join in.

Even Drake Strong himself let out a short rumble of laughter before he said, "We'll see how daring she is when it's time to climb the mountain or shoot down the zip line. How about exploring a cave, Miss Reynolds?"

"I've been exposed to far more intimidating circumstances, Mr. Strong. I'm sure I can handle anything you have to offer," Maggie defended herself with much more confidence in her voice than she felt. Even though the thought of gliding down a mountain on a cable, high above the ground, made her queasy, she refused to admit it. She remained undecided about crawling around in a dark, dusty cave. She'd have to try it in order to know how she felt about that one. Drake's voice cut into her thoughts.

"We'll be spending two weeks together," he addressed her directly. "Formalities are not necessary Maggie. Call me Drake."

She appreciated his attempt at civility, even if it did come a bit late. Her irritation eased, if only slightly. "Drake," she agreed and inclined her head in acceptance.

"Now for the rules," Drake spoke to the entire group. "Considering the potential dangers of my remote mountain resort, it's very important you follow my simple rules. Number one. No one goes anywhere alone." He looked pointedly at Maggie before he directed his focus on each of the other guests in turn. "Number two. As different situations arise, what I say goes. Period." He lifted a stack of papers and fanned them out. "I have documents for each of you to sign. You must agree to my terms and conditions before we leave for the cabins. You're also required to sign a waiver of liability for any unforeseen injuries. You do your part in staying safe and following my rules, and I'll do my part in keeping you out of harm's way."

The white-haired, older woman spoke up, "Oh dear. You make it sound so dangerous." Her aged hand clasped around her husband's arm.

Maggie tried to recall the woman's name, and her irritation resumed, as she blamed Drake for not being able to remember.

"It's not if you follow my rules and use common sense. There's nothing to be worried about, Annie."

"Oh, I'm not worried, son. I'm excited." Her lips parted to reveal a pair of even white teeth. "By the time you reach my age, not much'll scare ya anymore. Besides, between my new wedding vows and this adventure, I feel young and alive again."

"That's good to hear."

Maggie stored away Annie's name. Three down, three to go. She looked at Annie's husband. Was his name Gary? Harold? It could be Ichabod as far as she knew. She drew a complete blank. Maybe Annie or one of the other guests would mention his name again later.

Maggie studied the woman who wore loads of jewelry on her body and a sour expression on her face. Then she looked at the woman's spouse who wore the shiny hair-gel and fidgeted in his seat. Maggie wracked her brain, trying to remember their names.

The distant rumble of an airplane caught her attention. As it became louder and louder, Maggie looked up and saw an itty-bitty plane barely skim the tree tops before it bounced and landed unceremoniously on the lake. The seaplane jostled and coughed as it made its way to the long dock that held their luggage. As the engine wheezed out and the pilot erupted from the plane, Drake gave a wave to the small, wiry man.

"It seems our transportation to the cabins has arrived."

Maggie instantly forgot her mission to remember names as her stomach dropped to her toes. She swallowed hard as she looked at the tiny seaplane. *No way.*

"We'll ride over two at a time, starting with the Remmimgs. The Rileys next, then the Marcus. I'll ride over with Maggie on the last trip. Each round trip will take approximately an hour."

He looked over at Maggie. "You'll have time to get your boots." Drake handed out the papers for each person to sign before they departed on their journey. The guests dispersed, and began to ready themselves for the trip, but Maggie kept her eyes trained on Drake.

Maggie stood and found her knees a bit weak as she walked over to him and said, "That's not a plane! That's...that's a tin can with wings!" She heard the outrage in her own voice. "You said there would be a choice of how to get to the cabins. By truck or by air. You said nothing about that..." she pointed to the tiny plane. "That deathtrap!"

The man had the nerve to chuckle. "And when did I tell you that?"

"In the brochure!" Maggie dug in her purse to find it again. "It says so right here."

He nodded his head. "Okay, but read the fine print." He pointed to a small disclaimer at the bottom of the page.

Maggie read it aloud. "Asterisk. Due to unforeseen difficulties, the mode of transportation may vary." She looked up at him with wide eyes.

"Well, you can always go to the spa resort."

She gathered up her nerves and asked, "Didn't I make it clear to you that I am going on this trip?"

"You made it clear before. Sounds like you're having second thoughts now."

"No second thoughts." She held her chin high.

"See you in a few hours then," he said and walked away, leaving Maggie to stare at his retreating back.

"Wait!" The desperation in her own voice made her cringe. "Why?"

"Why what?" Drake stopped walking but didn't turn around. His head dropped down and a sigh heaved his shoulders.

"Why can't we take the truck?" she asked as she came up alongside him.

He lifted his head and directed his eyes to hers. "If you must know, a storm passed through here a few days ago and knocked down several large trees. Many of which are now blocking the only road leading to my property."

"Oh." Her hope deflated. How could she argue with that?

"Now, if you'll excuse me. I need to help Annie and Larry into the plane." Drake left her staring after him.

Larry. Maggie stored away his name for future reference as she looked in the direction of the plane. Annie and Larry actually looked happy as they climbed into it. Was she the only one going on this retreat without a death wish? She shook her head and prayed she would survive long enough to actually go on her vacation.

Chapter Two

Maggie liked the first pair of hiking boots she tried on. She even found the mosquito repellant, gloves and long underwear without a problem. But, she didn't see any motion sickness pills anywhere. She went to the counter in Jenkins' Country Store and looked at the GPS units displayed on the wall behind it. She cringed at the prices.

The clerk behind the counter moseyed over and asked, "Can I help you miss?"

Maggie looked up and smiled at the attractive older man. "Yes. I can't seem to find any motion sickness pills. Could you tell me where to find them?"

"Sorry. We don't carry 'em."

"What about any of the other shops?"

"Nope. They don't either. I'm sure of it."

No motion sickness pills? Maggie grabbed the solid oak counter as the room tilted. A bead of sweat rolled down her temple as nausea teased her turbulent stomach. She prayed she would be able to handle the duration of the flight without throwing up. How embarrassing would that be? She knew she hadn't made a good impression on Drake Strong and knew it would only make matters worse if she threw up on him.

"Anything else I can get for you?" The man nodded at the GPS units, completely oblivious to her dire situation.

"No thank you. I'm done shopping." She looked at the GPS units again and let out a nervous laugh. "I would still get lost if I had one of those gadgets."

His smile showed a touch of empathy. His close-cropped, dusty, gray hair looked like ash as sunlight filtered through from the window behind him.

"I'm Jenkins." He held out his hand.

"Maggie Reynolds." She politely shook his hand.

"I can teach you how to use one," he said and leaned closer to her on the counter with a devilish grin.

Maggie backed up an inch and began to shake her head when a familiar voice spoke up behind her. "She's not interested in you old man."

"Drake." Jenkins stood tall, looked past Maggie's shoulder and nodded. He had the decency to look chagrined. "How would you know?"

"She's one of mine. I know she'd have better sense than to get near the likes of you," Drake said as he put a pack of batteries on the counter next to Maggie. A small draft of air flowed with him as he settled in beside her, bringing with it a hint of spicy aftershave. He leaned an elbow on the counter and faced her.

Maggie stood straighter, wary of the tone of the conversation. She glanced back and forth between the two men, ready to put an end to the quarrel. When they both broke into a smile, relief flooded through her. She'd had enough confrontations in the past few days to last her a lifetime.

"One of mine?" Maggie asked and turned to face Drake. She leaned her elbow on the counter opposite his, tilted her head sideways and waited for a response.

"Yeah. You signed the paper. You're mine for two weeks."

An unexpected warmth spread through Maggie as the words soaked in. Even though she knew they weren't meant to be personal, they felt personal. Her cheeks warmed as she watched him carefully. His eyes remained focused on hers for several moments as he studied her. His lips turned up on one side, exposing a dimple.

She quickly turned back to face Jenkins. "Do you take debit cards?"

"Sure do."

Maggie paid for her purchases and thanked Jenkins. Gathering her bags and purse, she pushed away from the counter and started to walk past Drake, but he stopped her with a firm hand on her arm.

"We'll be leaving in about fifteen minutes. Be ready."

"But the plane isn't back yet."

"It'll be here," he said with unwavering confidence.

Maggie nodded and tried to sound confident herself. "Then I'll be ready." She walked away with jittery nerves and the residual warmth on her arm where Drake had touched her.

****

Drake turned to watch Maggie walk out of the store. Vitality radiated around her in waves and her full, auburn hair bounced with each step she took. Her slender appearance brought out natural protective instincts in Drake, instincts that he didn't want to have. However, she had already shown him that she wasn't as breakable as she appeared to be. A small bud of admiration had taken root when she had courageously stood up to his abrasiveness.

"She's a pretty one," Jenkins spoke up, drawing Drake's attention back to his friend.

"She's trouble." Drake stood tall and scooted the batteries closer to Jenkins.

"Maybe, but her husband is one lucky man." He glanced over to the doorway.

"That's just it. She's not married."

Jenkins gave a light cackle and looked at Drake again. "This a first for your resort?"

"It is. Most people understand how the resort is set up. They know not to come alone."

"Why did you let her make a single reservation?"

"I didn't. She was supposed to be a newlywed. Then she shows up alone and determined to go anyway."

"You know, it's not the end of the world if you have a lone guest."

Drake ran a hand over his face and shook his head. "Yeah well, I have better things to do than to baby-sit a woman with personal problems."

"Is that what she told you? That she had personal problems?"

"No. But whatever happened, she's here alone and that means she's carrying baggage along with her. She's trouble," Drake reiterated with a heavy sigh.

"Maybe you could use some trouble. Shake things up a bit."

"I don't like to be shaken. I like my life the way it is."

Jenkins rang up the batteries and put them into a small, brown bag. "She's reserved around you."

"She should be." Drake paid Jenkins and headed out. "Catch you in two weeks."

"Don't be too hard on her," Jenkins called after him. Drake lifted a hand in reply.

Drake walked out of the store with a little more than he intended to. He only wanted batteries, not advice. Jenkins' words followed him out the door along with a little pang of guilt. He had been hard on the woman. He rounded a corner and saw her pacing the shoreline, warily studying the seaplane as it docked once again. He stopped and leaned on a nearby tree to watch her.

Something more than the seaplane ride had her in a tizzy. She had been tense and nervous before she had even known about the seaplane. He had seen the desperation in her eyes when she'd tried to convince him to let her go. That alone had kept him from sending her away.

He watched as she ran her hands through her

mass of shoulder length auburn waves and then clench them into white knuckled fists as she walked. She couldn't seem to stand still. Just when she paused for a moment, she'd start out again. She went back and forth, wearing a path in the dirt with her new boots.

He gave a reluctant smile. At least she had taken his advice and bought herself a good pair of hiking boots. As he studied her, a part of him wanted to ease her fears and help calm her, the other part still wanted to send her packing. But he'd told her she could go, and he always kept to his word. He wouldn't compromise his integrity just because he was afraid he might end up liking her. Drake pushed away from the tree and picked up a crate of supplies, wondering just how much trouble Maggie Reynolds would prove to be.

****

"Ready to go?" Drake's deep voice vibrated Maggie's already raw nerves. He swept passed her on the dock carrying a large, wooden crate. He set it down and turned to her, dusting off his hands. "I'll get your luggage." His last words faltered when he saw her face. "Are you okay?" He asked as he stepped closer to her. Concern lined his features which made him look a little more human.

Maggie nodded quickly. Her eyes darted from the plane back to Drake's questioning eyes.

"You're not going to pass out on me are you?"

Maggie shook her head and swallowed hard but said nothing.

Drake put his hand on the small of her back and gently urged her to move toward the seaplane. "It'll be okay. I've flown with Harley hundreds of times, and we've never had a problem. I'll be right there with you."

Maggie stopped suddenly and looked into Drake's eyes. She managed to squeak out the words, "Harley? His name is Harley?"

Drake chuckled warmly. "He's a good pilot. Come on. I'll introduce you."

He continued to urge her forward but fear burdened her feet. Every step she took required more effort than the last. When the pilot came into view, Maggie tried her best to be polite and shook his hand when he offered it.

"Little 'fraid of flying ma'am?" Harley asked.

"W-why do you ask?"

"Just a hunch. You're hand is as cold as a lizard."

Maggie looked down and took her hand back. She produced a fake smile. "I'm fine. I'm just used to planes that are a little bit...bigger."

"No worries ma'am," Harley drawled. "My Piper has just undergone a complete overhaul." He patted the yellow and white fuselage like a beloved pet.

"Overhaul?" Maggie felt the blood drain from her face down to her toes. "Why did it need an overhaul?"

"Well, she had a lot of hours on her and one of the pontoons sprung a leak."

The world began to spin and she was sure she'd faint. She knew she must have appeared whiter than the seaplane's refurbished pontoons.

"It'll be all right." Drake's reassurance helped restore some of the color in her cheeks until he looked at the pilot and asked, "No stunts this trip, okay Harley?"

Maggie stopped breathing. Her eyes sought Drake and she found amusement sparkling in his eyes.

"Just kidding."

When she found her breath again she stammered, "Very funny."

Before she lost her nerve, she climbed into the back of the seaplane. She prayed fervently to survive. Of all the plane crashes she had ever heard about most of them were tiny planes like this one.

Please Lord, let us make it, and keep me from losing my breakfast.

Drake loaded the suitcases and climbed into the front passenger side. Harley did some checks on the plane before he climbed in.

"All set Miss Reynolds?" Harley turned to look at her. He then looked at Drake and said, "Hand her the bag."

Mortification swept through Maggie when Drake turned and reached back with a white, plastic lined barf bag. She felt like she could hurl at any given moment but she thought she'd had hid it better than that. She groaned and reluctantly took the bag. She pressed her forehead to the side window and closed her eyes hoping against hope they would land safely and she could return the bag, unused.

The plane's single engine roared to life as Harley and Drake carried on a conversation. She peeled her eyes open to watch the two men in the front who looked completely at ease. She wished she could siphon some of their confidence into her rapidly beating heart.

Maggie cringed when the plane sped along the water. They headed straight for the line of trees on the other side of the lake. She grabbed the seat and braced herself. At the last second she squeezed her eyes shut and prepared for impact. When nothing happened, she peeked out of the corner of one eye. She let her head fall back onto the seat when she saw they had cleared the trees. They may make it after all.

The scenery outside the window took her breath away, unfortunately so did her nausea. Maggie leaned forward to ask, "How long is this trip?"

"Just a few more minutes. It can take up to a few hours by the winding road, but by air? Not long at all," Drake answered and turned to look at her. "Are you okay?"

She quickly nodded her head and gave a weak smile. "Kinda."

"Remember the bag."

Heat rose up her face again. "I remember," she said as she flopped back in her seat.

Harley said, "Don't feel bad ma'am. 'Bout half of my passengers end up using one of them."

Maggie met his eyes and nodded. "Somehow, that doesn't make me feel any better right now." She had to stop talking. She felt like if she opened her mouth again, a lot more than words would come out.

"There's the lake." Drake pointed to the right of the plane.

Relief spread through Maggie until she peered down at a small patch of water. She found her voice again in a hurry. "That's a lake? It looks like a pond. Are you sure…"

"I'm sure. It looks narrow, but it's long. Don't worry."

Don't worry. Yeah right.

Maggie grasped her seat and held on for dear life. Harley brought the nose down and her stomach dipped along with the plane. Her sweaty palms slid on the vinyl seat as she swallowed the bile that rose in her throat. The plane bounced and jarred as it skimmed and landed on the lake. Finally, it slowed to a crawl as Harley expertly directed them to the dock.

Maggie managed to keep from using the bag, but she felt like she was the one needing an overhaul now. She climbed out of the tin can, silently thanking God for the safe trip. When she stood on the dock, she felt like her insides still rolled and tumbled with the turbulence. She stumbled to the side and felt a steady arm capture her waist.

"Maybe you'd better take a seat on the picnic table," Drake said as he ushered her to the wooden table.

Maggie felt fatigue claim her limbs, and she took

refuge in the solid strength of Drake's arm around her waist. She flopped to the bench seat and mumbled, "Thanks." Drake placed his warm hand on her neck, coaxing her to plant her face into her knees with gentle pressure.

"It will help your nausea if you keep your head down."

"I hope so. I feel miserable," she admitted as she leaned her forehead on her knees.

"Wish you had taken me up on the spa resort offer?"

She didn't know if he was serious or teasing her. Considering her frayed nerves, Drake's statement sent a spiral of irritation rocketing to the surface once again. She shook her head from side to side and instantly regretted the movement as the nausea taunted her. She stilled her head and moaned, "Go away."

His hand left her neck immediately. "Stay there until you can walk." Drake's voice became edgy, impatient. "Your cabin is the farthest one out. It's unlocked. You'll find the key inside." His gruff statement held no warmth. Maggie could hear his departure as his boots ground on tiny bits of gravel.

The glimpse of kindness she had seen in Drake instantly disappeared with her demand for him to go away. A part of her wished she hadn't said it as a slight bit of disappointment ran through her. She could almost like Drake when he was being nice. But, his kindness didn't last long enough for her to tell.

Maggie sat still and stared down at the ground through the small space between her knees. She watched a row of ants march their way to a feast of crumbs under the table. A breeze rustled the leaves and occasionally she heard distant voices travel past her and echo against the forest of trees.

She had only caught a glimpse of the resort before her head hit her knees, not enough to really know what it looked like. So far, she knew it had a long, skinny lake and ants. Curiosity won out over nausea, and she lifted her head from her lap. So far so good. Maggie sat up straighter to look around, only to have a cold, wet washcloth pressed to her face.

"I could tell by the looks of you when you stepped off that plane you could use some of my tea," a woman's voice explained as she released the washcloth.

Maggie spotted the rosy cheeked, slightly plump woman before she caught the soothing aroma of the tea. Dimples appeared on the woman's cheeks, and Maggie's heart lurched. The dimples looked oddly familiar.

"I'm Aunt Camelia. Everyone calls me Aunt Cammie, though." The woman's warm smile completely melted Maggie's annoyance away.

"Thank you. I'm Maggie Reynolds," she said as her muscles relaxed.

"I know."

Maggie lifted her eyebrows.

"News travels fast in a resort as small as this one. Not much'll get past me, I'll tell ya that now."

"Are you a guest too?"

Bright laughter came from deep in her throat. "No dear. I'm Drake's aunt. I work for him."

That explains the familiar dimples, Maggie thought.

Drake's aunt gestured to a large building just to the right of the picnic table. Maggie saw a sign above the door, proclaiming it to be Aunt Cammie's Kitchen.

"I do the cooking. Three square meals a day. There's a dining table inside that has a great view of the lake. But on nice days I'll serve up the food out here on this table." She patted the long picnic table. "I serve up at eight, twelve and five," she said as she scooted the tea closer to Maggie. "Here, drink up now. If you're late, you can find your plate in the fridge. Otherwise, snacks are in the cupboard."

"Sounds good." Maggie saw a deep rooted kindness in the woman's demeanor. "So, you're Drake's aunt? I see the family resemblance. You have the same dimples as Drake."

The woman seemed overly pleased with her assessment. "Yes, I like to think of him as the boy I never had." Maggie detected a passing glimpse of sadness reflected in her eyes. Aunt Cammie rattled on, "He's not a boy anymore is he? I heard you're here alone, is that right?"

Uh oh. Maggie recognized the matchmaking twinkle in Aunt Cammie's eyes.

"At first, my Drake can seem a little...rough around the edges. But I tell you, my dear, he's got a heart of gold."

"Really? I haven't seen it yet."

She chuckled. "Give him enough time and you will."

"No offense but I'm not here to see Drake's heart."

Aunt Cammie leaned over and patted Maggie's shoulder. "Breakups are tough on young'uns like you. But you'll get back on your feet soon enough."

"How did you know? Oh yeah. Small resort. Word travels fast."

"Yes." Aunt Cammie smiled. "Well, I'll be on my way. See you at supper."

Maggie nodded her head and smiled even though the thought of food made her want to retch. She hoped the tea would work its magic on her stomach so she could join the others for supper. Drake had already made her feel like an outcast, if she missed the first meal, she'd feel even more like one.

Maggie took a good look around her for the first time. At first glance, she could see a lake with a dock, a fire-pit, five cabins, Aunt Cammie's Kitchen, a storage shed and trees. Lots and lots of trees.

When she gave the area another, longer look she saw and felt something beyond that of the obvious. She took in the details of her surroundings and noticed the trees teemed with creatures, some she could see, others she could only hear. She saw squirrels jump from branch to branch, a lizard skitter under a pile of leaves, and a lone eagle circling high over her head.

Maggie smelled the fresh air and looked at the sparkling blue lake. The dock reached out into the water and had a floating platform on the end of it. Two recliners sat side by side on the platform which reminded her she had joined a couples retreat, making her even more uncomfortable. She saw a fish jump near the dock, sending a series of ripples across the placid lake.

The serenity of the entire area contrasted with the long range of emotions churning deep within her. She took a deep breath, trying to absorb some of the peace nature provided as she continued to study her surroundings.

The cabins held a rustic appeal yet had modern touches. Each cabin had its own gravel path leading up to a set of wide steps. Solar lampposts stood high above the ground in front of each cabin, while smaller solar lights lined the walkways.

The steps led up to covered porches that stretched as wide as the cabins. Flowerpots adorned each porch, no doubt courtesy of Aunt Cammie. Maggie tried to imagine Drake filling the terra-cotta pots with petunias and keeping them watered. The thought of the large, manly-man fiddling with flowers brought a smile to her lips.

She saw wooden rockers on each porch. Had Drake carved them? Now that she could imagine. She noticed each rocker had a partner, reminding her again that she didn't. The sudden disappointment caught her off guard, and she drew in a deep breath. She forced her thoughts to change and focus on the present. She squared her shoulders in determination and stood from the bench. The tea had worked magic, her nausea had faded away.

Maggie folded the washcloth and left it on the table for Aunt Cammie along with the empty tea cup, happy to know that someone, besides Cyndi, welcomed her here.

"You'd better get settled and ready for supper. It's getting close to five and Aunt Cammie always has the meal ready on time."

Maggie almost jumped out of her new boots. She twisted around and saw Drake. "I didn't see you behind me."

"You should be more alert. I could have been a bear," he growled as he carried the crate of supplies past her.

"You are a bear, Mr. Strong," Maggie spoke loud and clear as she placed her hands on her hips.

Drake immediately stopped and dropped the crate to the ground. He stood tall and held his back rigid to her for a moment. When he turned to face her, he had a smile on his lips that didn't quite reach his eyes. He slowly stepped toward her, and she had to make a conscious effort not to retreat.

"I should warn you, Maggie," he stepped within the realm of her personal space before continuing. "As your host, I can make your stay here pleasurable, or I can make it a living nightmare. Which do you prefer?"

Maggie closed the gaping hole in her mouth to speak. "P-probably the former, Mr. Strong. I mean Drake. I apologize. My runaway mouth has gotten me into trouble more than once."

His gaze lowered to her lips. "I don't doubt that for a minute." As his eyes traveled back to hers, they turned a shade darker.

She moistened her dry lips. He watched.

She fought hard to find her voice. "I've been a bit

on edge, lately. With all that's been happening..." her voice trailed off. "Maybe we can start over."

"You're mistaken. There is no *we*." He turned and picked up the crate, walking away without a backward glance.

Chapter Three

Maggie lugged her exhausted body up the steps to the cabin. Her suitcases thudded behind her with each step she climbed. The stressful day combined with the past few weeks loomed over her like a menacing shadow. She had made it to the cabin, despite the resistance from Mr. Strong, despite the fear of flying in a tin can, and despite her broken heart and shattered dreams. If she could make it this far, Maggie reasoned, she could continue a bit further.

She wanted to find something to complain about to bring Drake Strong down a notch. She hoped to find a leaky faucet, a toilet that wouldn't flush, or at the very least a dust bunny inside the cabin. But, when she walked through the door, she saw only immaculate and luxurious accommodations.

The spacious room had a living area with an inviting sofa facing a fireplace with wood already stacked in a neat pile, ready to use. A mahogany desk with a decorative lamp on it, sat to the far right by a window.

Maggie stepped further into the room and pulled her suitcases in behind her before she shut the door. She examined the queen size bed that rested beyond the living area. Its fluffy comforter appeared warm and inviting. As she got closer, she spotted a piece of chocolate waiting for her on each of the pillows. It took all of her willpower not to collapse onto the welcoming bed and drift off into oblivion. But, if she did that, she may not find something to complain about. So she kept searching the cabin.

The only other door in the room led to a spacious

bathroom that took her breath away. A Jacuzzi tub nestled in the corner of the modern and luxurious room. It looked like a mirage, so she went over and touched it to make sure it was real. The cool, smooth curves of the tub led down to more than a dozen jets deep in the bottom. It called to her. This time she gave in.

She ignored Drake's warning about being late for supper and turned the water on to fill the tub. Before she got too complacent, however, she searched the sink's faucet for a leak. But, it didn't drip. Not even once. She flushed the toilet and couldn't find anything wrong with it. Next she checked under the bed for dust bunnies. Not one could be found.

She sat on her knees for a moment beside the bed and looked around. Touches of color splashed the walls and furniture, making the otherwise earth-toned room inviting and cozy. It looked like Drake Strong had gone out of his way to make his resort a comfortable and appealing place to stay.

Maggie unfolded herself from the floor and readied herself for her bath. She climbed into the tub and let the hot, pulsating water relax her muscles as she sank neck deep into the water. Her thoughts turned to the mystifying resort owner. Why would someone who seemed so rugged and irritable go out of his way to make his guests extra comfortable? As her thoughts wandered, the warm water soothed her tense muscles. Afraid of falling asleep in the tub, she reluctantly turned off the jets after a few minutes and opened the drain. Her former irritation swirled away down the drain with the retreating water.

Maggie found a soft, huggable robe hanging on the back of the bathroom door. She pulled it on and snuggled into it. Drake's attention to detail surprised her and a budding respect for the resort's rugged owner began to take form in her. With her mood vastly improved, Maggie decided to change her approach to Drake. So far, standing up for herself only seemed to aggravate the man. She decided to compliment him instead of trying to bring him down a notch to see what kind of reaction that would stimulate.

Not that I care what he thinks anyway, Maggie assured herself. But he did have a point when he said he could make her stay here miserable. She didn't doubt for a second that he would too, if he was so inclined.

She padded into the living area, enjoying the feel of the plush carpet under her bare toes. She looked at the bed and lost all willpower. She drifted over to it, snatched up the chocolates and ate them both at the same time. She pulled the covers back and slipped into the sheets.

"Just for a few minutes," she said aloud to herself. The sheets smelled as clean as the forest air and the pillow felt like it had been custom made for her.

Maggie curled up into a ball, swallowed the last of the chocolate and closed her eyes. She tensed as she began to think of Nathan and her desperate circumstances. As her fear threatened to return, she tucked her head down deeper into the soft pillow and prayed, *I know You have a plan for me, Lord. Please help me to know your will and follow your path.* An image of the footprints in the sand came to her, reminding her of God's promise to always be with her. A much needed sense of peace came over her and she immediately dropped into a deep, restful sleep.

****

Drake brought the axe down harder than he had intended to. He had been letting his frustration out on the logs for over a half an hour, yet he still felt the need to chop the wood into smithereens. He swung the axe again and heard the wood splinter as it cracked in two. Each half of the log flew in opposite directions.

He stood still for a moment as he looked at the firewood. His sour thoughts kept his ill-tempered mood fueled. He liked to be in control. That included keeping a tight rein on his temper, which he discovered today, would be extremely difficult around his new guest. Maggie Reynolds tested his patience more today than anyone had dared in a long time.

Drake set the axe down and positioned a larger, more challenging log into place. He placed a wedge in a crack of the log and raised the sledge hammer up over his head. He slammed it down, metal met metal and the resulting pressure tore the wide log into more manageable pieces.

What had she been thinking coming alone? Just in case his brochure hadn't been clear enough, he had made it crystal clear to her in person that she didn't belong. Yet, she had insisted.

Maggie's image sprang to his mind again. The desperation showed through her eyes, just as her anger had when he had been intentionally rude to her. Any sane person would see his irritation and run. But not Maggie. His curtness only seemed to get her ire up and make her dig the heels of her new boots in deeper. He speculated on the reasons behind her desperation as he put the sledge hammer down and picked up the axe again. He chopped at the smaller logs until he had worked enough energy out of his system to calm down a few degrees.

He set the tools in their proper places and gathered the logs. He stacked them neatly into piles as he decided how best to handle her. If she would keep to herself and stay out of trouble, things might work out okay. But seeing how her temper flared when he suggested she be more alert for bears, he seriously doubted she would. She obviously hadn't taken him seriously about the dangers out here.

Drake stood and carried a few logs to the fire-pit, readying it for the introductory campfire. He always made it a point to gather everyone together for the first night to explain, in detail, the precautions that needed to be taken in the wilderness.

At five o'clock, Drake watched the guests gather at the picnic table after Aunt Cammie rang the old-fashioned supper bell. The guests had promptly arrived, except Maggie. Drake didn't care who ate dinner and who didn't. As long as the food had been offered, his responsibility had been fulfilled. But, he did require that each guest be at the campfire on the first night. He had made that fact clear in the brochure.

When supper had been served and cleaned up, and Maggie still hadn't appeared, Drake had to consciously hold back his flaring temper. Apparently, he thought as he stalked to her cabin, she had deemed his request for her presence at the campfire that night as unimportant.

He glanced behind him and saw the other guests settled at the campfire. His irritation mounted as he climbed the steps to her cabin two at a time. He rammed his fist into the door, knocking three times before he shouted, "Maggie!"

He heard faint movements then a crashing sound before the door opened to reveal startled, wide brown eyes peering at him. Drake looked down past Maggie's eyes and lost his breath as he spotted the robe he provided for his guests wrapped around her small figure. Standing there in the white fluffy attire, Maggie looked innocent and somewhat manageable. Her vulnerability showed through in her disoriented state as she blinked her eyes and ran a hand through her hair.

She clasped the ends of the robe tighter around her chest and asked, "What's wrong?"

Her sleepy voice threatened to undo his tight

resolve. With her defenses down, her soft voice seemed almost timid and shy. How could he yell at her for being late now? He searched for words, came up empty and stood before her, speechless.

Maggie looked past his shoulder and asked, "Is it getting dark already? I didn't mean to sleep so long. I must have been exhausted. Is it time for the campfire?"

Drake nodded.

"Ok. I'll be right out."

"Hurry, everyone's waiting for you," he said gruffly. He stalked way, annoyed at his intense reaction to her vulnerable state.

****

Maggie knew she would be the last to arrive. She had berated herself for oversleeping as she hastily freshened up and slid on her clothes. She ignored the grumbles in her stomach and approached the campfire with caution. Drake had been abrupt with her yet again and she suddenly doubted she would ever be able to squeeze onto his good side, even with well-intended compliments.

Her doubts escalated as she approached the group of guests seated around the roaring campfire and spotted Drake. He sat on top of the picnic table, positioned as if he didn't have a care in the world, but his venomous eyes betrayed his indifference. He made no move to disguise his contempt as he watched her slip into the only available chair.

"Hi Maggie," Cyndi said as she twiddled her fingers at her.

She nodded her head and gave a smile. "Hey Cyndi." Maggie looked to the rest of the group. Dillon's sparkling eyes locked with hers and he gave a brief nod. Annie and Larry leaned close to each other cheery-faced, looking as if they were ready to take on the world. The woman in her fifties sat staring off into the darkness with her arms crossed. Her husband stared at his shoes while shuffling them around impatiently.

Maggie jumped when Drake spoke abruptly, "Now that we are all finally here, we'll get started." He surveyed the group of guests and stood in front of them. "As you know, we're far enough from civilization for us to be considered the outsiders here. When we encounter any wild animals, we must respect the fact that we are on their turf. There are a few precautions you can take to make your stay here a relaxing and enjoyable one." Drake glanced at Maggie and continued, "Black bears are common in this area. It's very important to keep a clean camp so we won't attract them. Keep all food in tightly stored containers when you go on hikes and never leave anything behind after a picnic. Around camp, make sure you leave no trash or food out after you eat."

Cyndi raised her hand as if in a classroom.

"Yes Cyndi?" Drake stopped and looked at her.

"Isn't it dangerous to eat outside then?"

Drake shrugged, "Not particularly. Bears come through here anyway, regardless of where we eat. The important thing is not to give them any motivation to return."

The man with the hair gel snorted. "We all know about bears, what else is there we need to know about?"

Drake looked at the man and answered, "Well, Stephen, snakes are commonplace as well. There are a variety of them around here, some are poisonous and some are not. But you should treat them as if they're all dangerous."

Maggie chewed on her bottom lip. She stored away Stephen's name, and as she did, she suddenly remembered his wife's name, Beverly. She felt triumphant now that she knew all of the guest's names. She looked at the edgy couple again. Beverly wore her usual tight expression and Stephen looked a little egotistical as he tilted his head at Drake.

Maggie wondered if Beverly and Stephen were

having serious marital problems or if they just needed a break from each other. The only time she saw them looking at each other was with scowls on their faces. Either way, she didn't understand why they would come out to a place like this where they couldn't get away from each other.

"Am I boring you Miss Reynolds?" Drake's words broke into Maggie's thoughts.

Maggie jumped slightly and returned her focus to him as she felt her face heat with embarrassment. She wondered what Drake had said that she missed. She looked around at all the eyes watching her.

"Of course not."

Drake continued as if she hadn't answered him, "They like to hide in tall grass and under rocks. I've found a few hiding under the firewood before too."

Dillon asked, "Have any of your guests been bitten?"

"Yes," Drake answered without elaboration.

Annie spoke up, "Oh, dear."

Drake looked at the older woman. "Don't worry, Annie. With proper treatment, most snake bites aren't lethal."

Maggie asked, "Most?"

Drake turned his eyes to her. "Yes. Most." Then he turned his focus to the rest of the group again. "You need to remember some things if you get bitten. First, stay as calm and still as possible and keep the area bitten lower than your heart. Second, send your partner to come and get me immediately. If I see the snake, I can identify if it's poisonous and if medical treatment is necessary. I have access to a phone in case we need to call for help."

"That's all? Shouldn't we slice the wound and suck out the venom?" Stephen asked.

Drake took a seat on top of the picnic table again and laced his fingers together. "No. Cutting the wound causes further injury and hasn't been proven to be effective."

"I hate snakes," Beverly admitted.

Maggie looked at her, astonished that the unyielding woman had just admitted a weakness.

"They don't usually come looking for a fight. If you come across any, leave them alone. Don't try to get a closer look at them. They usually only strike if they feel threatened," Drake informed them.

Maggie asked, "What about putting ice on it? Wouldn't that slow the venom from going through your bloodstream?"

He shook his head. "Doing that could also be harmful."

"Besides bears and snakes, what should we look out for?" Cyndi asked.

"Any kind of wild animal has potential to harm you. Remember, you're on their land. We're all visitors in the wilderness."

"You sound like a conservation brochure," Stephen complained.

Drake looked at Stephen. Amusement touched his eyes as he said, "I'm glad you've read that type of literature before. It could come in handy." He dismissed Stephen and said to the group, "Use your common sense, stay with your partner and you'll be fine. You'll find each of the scheduled group events I have planned posted on the bulletin board in the inside dining area. Each activity is weather permitting. It's your choice if you'd like to go or not. But, as I said before…"

"No one goes anywhere alone. And no one stays here alone," Maggie finished for him.

"I'm glad I've made myself clear."

"What about Aunt Cammie? If she's here, I can hang around with her. Right?" Maggie asked.

Drake shook his head. "It's not her job to baby-sit. If everyone else wants to try cave exploring or the zip line, you have to go too."

Maggie clenched her jaw. *Baby-sit?* So now she needed a baby-sitter? Resentment burned her throat and she retorted, "As I said before, I'm sure I can handle anything you have to offer."

"We'll see about that."

Their eyes locked in a battle of will. Maggie refused to even blink and she suddenly felt like a child having a staring contest as he stared back at her. She willed herself to keep her eyes open, but a gust of wind made her blink. She saw Drake's mouth curve up momentarily before he turned his focus to the group again.

"Enjoy your stay here. Let me know if you need anything."

Maggie gritted her teeth and thought, *how about a new host?*

Chapter Four

After Drake finished with his instructions, the guests lingered at the campfire for a few minutes, casting their own opinions about the dangers that mother-nature had to offer. Maggie noticed most of the guests showed excitement about experiencing a little bit of danger, as if the idea of it put an exciting spin on an otherwise monotonous existence.

Beverly slipped away from the rest of the group and headed down to the dock. Maggie watched as she sat alone for a few minutes. She waited to see if Stephen would follow, but he seemed too engrossed in a conversation about mountain lions to notice his wife's absence.

Maggie debated whether to go speak to the woman or not. Even though she thought she would probably be turned away, she felt pulled in Beverly's direction. She silently left the group and walked down to the dock. She prayed as she walked, *Lord, please let me know what to say to her*. She cleared her throat to alert Beverly of her approach.

"Hi Beverly," Maggie offered an opening as she sat in the chair next to her.

Beverly cut her eyes at her before looking back into the distance without a reply.

Maggie adjusted herself in the chair, uncomfortable with the woman's gesture. But something deep inside kept her from walking away. She sat and waited. The crickets and tree frogs chirped a chorus in the forest as a slight breeze blew the fresh scent of the lake across the area. Maggie took in a deep breath and nearly choked on it when Beverly finally spoke.

"I suppose you think I'm a stuffy, old nag don't you?"

Maggie barely kept her shock concealed. "Not at all."

"Then what you do think? I know you have an opinion. Everyone does."

"I think you've been hurt so many times and for so long that you've built up a fortress to protect yourself." Maggie saw the surprise in Beverly's eyes before she looked away.

A few minutes later Beverly said, "I suppose you've been hurt too."

Maggie took her comment as an affirmative that she had guessed right. "Hasn't everyone? In some form or another anyway."

Beverly's head whipped around. "Yeah. But you don't know what I've been through." She snipped and stood. "Do yourself a favor and never get married." She trudged away, concealing every ounce of emotion she had just showed Maggie.

Maggie sat alone, mulling over Beverly's words. She wondered if Stephen was as egotistical as he appeared, and what had happened in their marriage to make Beverly so bitter. Had Stephen cheated on her? As she contemplated the situation, she decided she didn't have enough information to draw any real conclusions.

She wondered what would have happened between her and Nathan had she not found him sleeping with another woman. Would she have married him and never known of his infidelity? Or would she realize it too late and turn out as miserable and bitter as Beverly? Maggie said a silent prayer, *Thank you Lord for letting me find out about Nathan's true character before making a huge mistake, and please help Beverly and Stephen have the help they need.*

As the campfire dwindled and the sounds of conversations dissipated, she cast a glance over her shoulder. Everyone had retired for the evening and Drake stood over the fire with a bucket of water. He doused the last of the flames, causing a burst of white smoke to erupt from the fire-pit. The darkness consumed his features as he set the bucket on the ground. He stood still for a moment, a dark shadow silhouetted in the night. Maggie wondered if he would come over to talk to her. She had her answer when he suddenly turned away and headed into the darkness.

The solar lights cast a dim glow in the otherwise pitch-dark night. Maggie searched for the moon, but clouds covered any sign of it. Her stomach complained, reminding her that she hadn't eaten since breakfast. She climbed out of the chair and carefully made her way off the dock and to Aunt Cammie's Kitchen.

The screen door creaked as she opened it and slammed shut behind her as she entered the building.

"Well, I was wondering if you'd show up, seeing as how you missed supper and all." Aunt Cammie's voice came from the left. Maggie looked to the open kitchen area and spotted her finishing up some dishes.

"This is a nice kitchen," she commented as she walked up to Aunt Cammie and picked up a dishcloth. "Sorry I missed dinner." She picked up a pan from the drying rack and began to wipe it dry with the cloth. "Don't you have a dishwasher?"

"Sure I do. Sometimes I just prefer doin' 'em by hand the old fashioned way." The woman's cheery smile sent a welcoming invitation Maggie's way. "You don't have to help sweetie. You're a guest remember?"

"I don't mind. Besides, I miss my kitchen."

"You like to cook?"

"No, I like to bake. It relaxes me. When I get stressed, I usually run for the kitchen and pull out the sugar and flour."

"Who eats it? You're too skinny to be eatin' it all yourself."

"My customers. I owned a bakery back in L.A. for a while."

"No kidding? Well just make yourself at home here 'cause that's the one thing I don't do. No ma'am. I can cook like you wouldn't believe, but don't ask me to bake. Maybe you could make us up some muffins or something for breakfast one day. If you get stressed that is..."

"I'd love too."

"That's good to hear." Aunt Cammie pressed a hand to her back and stretched her muscles. "I told Drake just the other day I need some help feeding his guests. I love to cook, but I ain't as young as I used to be." She sat on a stool and added, "Drake will get someone in here to help as soon as he figures out where he's gonna put 'em."

"Where do you stay?"

"Oh, Drake set me up in the back there." She indicated a door at the back of the kitchen. "Grab yourself some leftovers and I'll show you."

A few minutes later, Maggie stood in the open doorway looking at a wide screen TV that dwarfed any other she had seen. A leather couch lined the wall opposite the enormous TV with a modern coffee table in front of it. She noticed a laptop computer in the far corner of the well-decorated room.

"Drake insists that I have the best of everything." Aunt Cammie seemed pleased with her nephew's coddling as she showed Maggie into the room. "You should have seen him trying to sneak that huge TV in here. It was a birthday present last year. He tried to surprise me but, as I always say, not much gets past me. I knew he was going after it when he left that morning."

"Do you get many channels?"

"Tons of them. It's hooked up to satellite. It

wasn't easy getting it way out here, but Drake made sure I got it. Sometimes he comes and watches his favorite television shows with me."

Maggie tried to imagine Drake sitting back and watching a game or a sitcom but came up short. "I suppose I have a narrow view of him. I can't imagine seeing him kicked back watching a movie."

"There's a lot more to my Drake than you've seen. As I said, he can seem a little rough at times, but deep inside he feels more than he wants anyone to believe. He's had a rough time of it. His mother died of cancer when he was twelve and I raised him from then on. To be honest, he pretty much raised himself, and he took it upon his own shoulders to look after me. I never did get married. It was just him and me. Eventually, he went off and joined the service. He was a Navy SEAL for several years. Boy did I worry about him in those days. Then again, I still worry about him now. I suppose I always will." She settled into a recliner that matched the leather sofa. "Please have a seat and eat up."

"Thanks." Maggie found a coaster and set her drink on the coffee table. She pulled the lid off of the container Aunt Cammie had given her. "This looks good." A part of her wanted to know more about Drake, but she couldn't bring herself to ask so she took a bite of the dinner. "It's delicious."

"Thanks. I always start the first night with burgers and tater salad. I don't want the guest to expect gourmet every night. I save my favorites for later on in the week so they don't get spoiled right off."

"That sounds like a good plan."

A brief knock sounded at the door. "It's me. Are you still up?" Drake's voice came through the door.

Maggie jumped and almost choked on the bite of potato salad she had just put into her mouth. She hadn't expected to see Drake again tonight.

"I'm up. Come on in."

He started to open the door and paused midway when he saw Maggie. She noticed the surprised look on his face before he looked at his aunt and said, "I didn't know you had company. I just wanted to check up on you. Did you get all of the supplies you needed?"

Aunt Cammie twisted in her chair to look at her nephew. "Sure did." She turned to wave in Maggie's direction. "Have a seat with us. Maggie and I are getting to know each other. You should join us."

Drake looked at Maggie as if getting to know her was the last thing he wanted. "Thanks, Aunt Cammie, but I've got work to do."

His eyes stayed on Maggie for a moment. Her mouth ran dry and she took a quick sip of her drink before saying, "I like my cabin." Maggie cleared her throat. "I'm impressed with how you decorated it, and the Jacuzzi is a really nice touch."

"I'm glad you approve," he said dryly.

Maggie wondered what it would take to get on Drake's good side. Apparently, her compliment hadn't fazed him because he turned his focus back to his aunt, dismissing her altogether. She shouldn't care what he thought of her, but for some reason she wanted to be accepted by him.

"We'll be leaving in the morning right after breakfast."

Maggie felt like she had missed out on some vital piece of information. "Leaving to go where?"

Drake folded his arms across his chest and took another step into the room. "That's right, you missed supper," he said as if he had forgotten. He looked down at her plate then met her eyes again. "Over the meal we discussed the first excursion. I'm leading an overnight hike starting early tomorrow. The information is on the bulletin board in the dining room. You should check it out each day in case the weather changes."

"How far is the hike?"

"All of that information is posted," Drake said dismissively and turned to leave.

Aunt Cammie spoke up, "Drake, would you be a dear and make sure Maggie gets back to her cabin safely? I'd hate for her to walk back alone and come across a bear her first night here."

Maggie sucked in a breath and tried not to drop her plate of food. "I'll be fine."

"Now dear. I'm sure Drake won't mind at all."

Maggie looked at him to see his reaction. His jaw clenched and he gave a reluctant nod. She doubted the wisdom of being alone in the dark with a man who obviously didn't care for her, but at the same time her instincts told her that he wouldn't hurt her. She had a glimpse of his kindness when he had encouraged her to get on the seaplane and again after the ride, when he helped her to the picnic table. A part of her wanted to see that side of him again.

"I'll wait outside while you finish eating," he said without meeting her eyes and left the room.

She didn't think she'd be seeing the kinder side of him again tonight. She suddenly lost her appetite as her nerves kicked in, but didn't want to appear rude so she took another bite of the burger.

Aunt Cammie looked chagrined as she explained, "I declare, my Drake's usually a little friendlier than that."

"He doesn't like me."

"Nonsense. He's been through a rough patch in the past few years. It's left him a bit ornery, but he doesn't dislike you. He may feel a bit threatened by you. But it's not my place to tell you about it. That'll be up to him."

"I can't imagine anyone being threatened by me. Especially not him. He looks like he has no problem taking care of himself," Maggie answered as she got up from the couch. "Thanks for dinner. I really appreciate it."

Aunt Cammie looked up at her and said, "It's my

pleasure. I'd get up but my back is aching a bit tonight." She stretched in her recliner, looking uncomfortable.

Maggie motioned for her to stay sitting. "Don't get up. I'll let myself out. Thanks again for dinner. Goodnight."

"Goodnight Maggie."

She shut the door behind her as she wondered what kind of rough patch Aunt Cammie had been talking about. Drake seemed so impenetrable it was hard to think of him as having a hard time with anything.

She quickly washed the plate and set it in the drainer before hurrying over to the bulletin board to check out the events. She scanned the calendar, not wanting to keep Drake waiting for her too long. Sure enough, she found tomorrow's excursion posted in the middle of the board. The information indicated tomorrow's hike would consist of a strenuous eight mile trail, winding up the mountain. The challenge gave Maggie a rush of excitement. If something like that couldn't get her mind off her troubles, then nothing would. She scanned the details of the trip and discovered they would be staying at an overnight camp and dinner would be provided. The next day, a zip line ride would carry them down the mountain and cut their hike back down to only a few miles.

A spike of trepidation coursed through her at the thought of dangling beneath a thin wire and hanging high off of the ground. She had seen people doing that sort of thing on television, but had never expected to have the opportunity to experience a ride like that herself. Her stomach flip-flopped at the knowledge she would be faced with it in the near future.

She noticed a caving trip listed for later on in the week, but couldn't bring herself to face the idea of crawling around in a dark hole just yet, so she turned and headed for the door. She paused for a moment before opening it as she looked wistfully at the kitchen. The thought of baking something comforted her, and she wished she had the time to do it. She promised herself she would bake something to help Aunt Cammie soon as she opened the door to leave.

She stepped outside and took a breath of the sweet and clean mountain air, trying to calm her nerves. She hadn't counted on being alone with Drake Strong tonight, even if it only involved a short walk to her cabin.

The cloud-covered night sky provided no illumination for Maggie to see by. With the campfire washed out, the solar lights provided the only light. A slight breeze rustled leaves and tree branches, causing dancing shadows in the night. Maggie's imagination began to soar. Her eyes darted from one shadow to the next, looking for anything that may cause her harm. She didn't see Drake anywhere and she shivered at the thought of having to walk back to the cabin alone. She suddenly wished her cabin wasn't the farthest one away.

Drake materialized from the deep shadows behind her. "Ready?"

Maggie jumped and said, "I didn't see you. I thought maybe you had gone on without me." His presence immediately calmed her fears of the ominous shadows and she turned her focus to the tall man standing beside her. The darkness hid his features, making it difficult for her to judge his current mood.

"I said I'd walk you back," Drake answered as if he never changed his mind. He began walking down the dimly lit pathway.

They passed by Stephen and Beverly's cabin first then Drake's cabin came into view. His looked much like the others, except a little more lived in.

He seemed to be content to walk in silence, but

Maggie felt uncomfortable without talking so she said the first thing that popped into her head, "Aunt Cammie told me you have a heart of gold."

"Do you believe her?"

Maggie shrugged her shoulders. "I suppose anything is possible." She turned to smile at him, hoping to ease the discomfort mounting between them. "I can tell she loves you very much."

Drake nodded but remained silent as they passed by Annie and Larry's cabin and then Cyndi and Dillon's. As they came up to her cabin, Drake stopped at the bottom of the porch steps. Maggie stopped with him.

Unwilling to let the strained silence continue into the next day she said, "Since I'll be here for the next two weeks, do you think we could call a truce?" She held her hand out for a shake. She suddenly felt exposed with her hand stuck out in mid-air as she waited for him to make a move. She hoped he didn't reject her.

Drake lowered his eyes to her hand. He seemed to contemplate whether to take her offer or not. He looked back into her eyes before he took her hand in his warm, firm grip. "I'll make you a deal. Prove to me you won't be any trouble and then we'll have a truce."

The feel of his strong, calloused hand covering hers made it hard for her to find the words to answer him. She pulled out of his grasp before asking, "How do I prove it to you?"

"Submit to my authority and stay out of trouble."

"Submit?" Maggie's ego erupted and her eyes widened.

Drake held up a hand. "Don't get defensive on me now. All I'm saying is that I'm in charge out here. If you do as I say, we won't have a problem."

"How many times are you going to tell me that?"

"As many as it takes."

"Are you always this difficult?"

"Not with those who follow the rules."

"And I've already broken the biggest rule, right? By coming here alone?"

"Something like that, yeah."

"Do you think coming here alone was easy for me? Do you think I wanted..." Maggie cut off her words before she said too much. "Listen. I debated for hours whether I should come here or not. I decided to take a chance and come. Why is that such a horrible thing to you?"

Drake rubbed a hand over his shadowed jaw and shook his head. "My rules are set for a reason, Maggie. They're not meant to be broken."

"Then why did you let me come?"

"I almost didn't."

"Why did you?"

"Because when you pleaded with me, I saw the desperation in your eyes," he said with a sigh.

"I'm surprised you cared."

He ignored her remark and asked, "Why are you so desperate to be here?"

Maggie hesitated before answering, "It's complicated." She stuffed her hands into her pockets and shrugged.

He crossed his arms over his chest. "I have a feeling everything involving you is complicated."

"Look, Drake. I don't know what you expect from me but I'm not a trouble-maker."

He ran his eyes over her. "Yes, you are. Whether you intend to be or not."

"What does that mean?"

"Never mind," he said as he shook his head.

So much for trying to smooth things over, Maggie thought. She let out a pent up breath and raised her hands in defeat. She shook her head and headed up the porch steps.

Drake called out before she reached the door, "Don't miss breakfast in the morning."

Maggie spun around when she reached the top step. "Is that a suggestion or one of your rules?" She never got a reply because he had already disappeared into the night.

Chapter Five

Maggie's calves screamed at her for the abuse she imposed upon them. Drake led the group up a winding trail that had some level areas, but mostly held a steady incline. It even became so steep at some points that he had built makeshift steps into the slope to make traveling up the mountain possible.

Her thighs soon joined in with her calves in their complaints. Her shins came in a close third and elevated her discomfort even further. *So much for the membership to the gym,* she thought. Even the hours she had spent on the stair climber machine hadn't prepared her for this rugged terrain. Even so, the strenuous hike exhilarated Maggie. Her senses came alive and her heart pumped to keep up with the extra demands her body placed on it as she explored the wonders of nature.

She glanced at Drake as he led the group. He walked as if his boots had springs in them as he propelled ahead with ease. Of course, he wouldn't have a problem. Accustomed to a lifestyle such as this, he could probably go twice the distance without breaking a sweat. She studied his movements and a surprising spark of admiration lit inside her.

Stephen and Beverly had chosen to remain behind at the cabins. Cyndi and Dillon leapt along with boundless energy. If it weren't for Annie and Larry taking up the rear, Maggie knew she'd be lagging behind as she began to feel older than her thirty-one years.

"We'll take a break here," Drake called from the front of the group. He stopped at a small clearing covered in knee-high grass. "Keep a look out for snakes as you settle in, they tend to like the cover of the tall grass."

A few boulders edged the clearing and Maggie chose to sit on the one with the smoothest surface. Her legs quivered in relief as she sank down on the hard granite. Annie and Larry settled on another boulder, and Cyndi and Dillon disappeared into the green grass.

"Go ahead and grab a snack. This'll be our last stop before we reach the overnight camping area."

Maggie took in a sharp breath. That's what she had forgotten. Food. Her stomach let out a low rumble of hunger when she saw Annie and Larry pull out a whole line of food items from their backpacks. She saw sandwiches, chips and cookies. They must have raided Aunt Cammie's cupboard before the hike. She couldn't tell what Cyndi and Dillon were eating, but she heard munching sounds coming from below the grass-line. Maggie thought of the jumbo sized chocolate chip cookies she used to make every day in her bakery and almost drooled.

She watched as Drake pulled out a bright red apple. She heard the crisp snap as his teeth tore a bite off of the core. She caught herself staring just in time to turn away before he looked at her. She pulled out her water bottle and took an unsatisfying swig from it. She knew a learning curve accompanied each new endeavor, but she didn't like how hard the lessons were turning out to be.

Disgusted with herself for being so ill-prepared, she stood and walked away to the opposite side of the clearing, hoping the smells and sounds of eating wouldn't assault her there. She slid down to the ground and leaned on an unfriendly rock. She scrunched and squirmed until she rested somewhat comfortably and pulled her knees up to her chest. She crossed her arms over her knees and rested her cheek on her forearms, resigned to wait through snack time at a distance.

As she studied a patch of yellow wildflowers, she heard footsteps approaching. An apple appeared in front of her, attached to long, sturdy fingers and a large hand. Maggie glanced up at Drake as he stretched out his arm and silently offered a fresh apple to her. She only waited a fraction of a second before accepting it.

"Thanks," she said with a small smile and took a bite. That simple, kind gesture brought tears to eyes.

Nathan had showered her with numerous, expensive gifts on a regular basis. But each gift had felt generic and impersonal. None of them compared to the single apple she held in her hands. Drake, the harsh and demanding lumberjack of a man, had seen her need and filled it without her having to ask.

Confused emotions bounced around inside her. Why hadn't she seen how emotionally detached Nathan had been to her? Why did she feel like crying all over Drake Strong's well-worn boots?

"It's just an apple." His words sliced through her thoughts.

She strained her neck up to look at him. He took another bite of his own apple and looked at her as if she had just lost her mind for tearing up over a simple piece of fruit. How could she explain that it wasn't the apple itself as much as it was the thought behind it?

"No, it's more than just an apple. Thank you, Drake."

"If you say so." He shrugged his shoulders and turned to walk away.

"How much farther is it?" Maggie asked between bites of the delicious fruit.

Drake stopped and turned around. "We're a little over halfway. Getting tired?" he asked with a smirk.

Maggie wouldn't admit it if her feet were about to fall off. "I'm fine."

"Good." He nodded and sauntered away.

When Drake called her back to the group, Maggie stood on her stiff legs and her muscles started hollering at her again. She walked steadily over to them, refusing to let her fatigue show through.

Annie and Larry stood together and gathered their things. Annie said, "Drake, we've decided to head back down. This is far enough for us."

"All right." Drake nodded. "You two make sure to stay together. We'll see you tomorrow afternoon."

Annie and Larry began their trek back down the hill, leaving Maggie, Cyndi, Dillon and Drake in the clearing.

"Anyone else want to follow them back down?" Drake asked while he re-tied one of his boots. He glanced at each of them in turn and waited for a reply.

Cyndi and Dillon shook their heads enthusiastically.

Dillon spoke up, "No. I can't wait for the zip line ride tomorrow."

"Me either." Cyndi gave a wide grin and jumped up and down a few times.

"I'm not giving up," Maggie answered.

Drake nodded. "Okay then. We'll be able to pick up the pace now. Let's go."

Maggie's heart lurched as they set off at a much faster pace than they had been traveling with Annie and Larry. Cyndi and Dillon had boundless energy and they easily kept up with Drake. Maggie wondered what kind of snack they had eaten in the clearing. Maybe some sort of super-sonic, energy booster bars.

Maggie sucked in deep, ragged breaths of air as they continued to climb. Drake glanced back a few times but continued at a brisk pace. Just when she thought her lungs were going to explode, Drake stopped abruptly and turned around to face her.

His eyes bore into hers and a scowl lined his mouth as he asked, "Do you have so much pride that you would rather collapse on this trail than to ask me to slow down for you?"

"I..." Maggie's voice gave out on her. She looked at Cyndi and Dillon who immediately ducked their heads and walked ahead until they were out of earshot.

Drake took a few steps toward her and blocked the trail with his body. He crossed his arms as he looked her over while waiting for a reply.

Maggie slowly caught her breath, but her heart continued to race under Drake's intense scrutiny. "I'm fine," she insisted with her head held high.

A humorless smile escaped his lips. "You know, you can tell a lot about a person from how they react to their environment and how they handle different situations that arise."

"Yeah, so what are you saying?"

He took a step closer and said, "I'm saying that you're either too full of pride to admit when you need something from someone, or your self esteem is so low that you don't feel like you deserve any accommodations."

Drake's words slammed into her. She shook her head and retreated a step.

"Don't back away from the truth Maggie," Drake said as he turned away and started to walk. He turned halfway back around as he walked and growled, "Next time, ask."

Maggie followed in silence. At first, her defenses raged in an internal sparring match with Drake as she thought of a dozen arguments to refute his statement. But as they continued their ascent on the trail, Drake's words sunk into her and weighed her down. Had she been too prideful to ask him to slow down? Or not confident enough in herself to ask for her own needs to be met?

Drake occasionally stopped and shared tidbits of

information with them about the types of trees they passed by or the wildlife they spotted. Other than those brief tourist-like moments, everyone remained silent. They crossed paths with a stream several times as it wound its way down the mountain, cascading over rocks and boulders on its decent. The soothing sound helped relax Maggie as she continued to climb.

When they finally arrived at the overnight camping area, she sighed in relief. The strains from the hike and from her emotional tug-of-war had taken their toll. She flopped on the picnic table and took note of her surroundings.

An L-shaped building sat at the far end of the clearing on the left with a fire-pit surrounded by a ring of large rocks on the ground. It looked much like the makeshift campgrounds she and her brothers made on the Texas ranch she had been raised on, all except for the surrounding mountain ranges.

Cyndi walked over to Drake and asked, "Is this as primitive as it looks? I don't suppose there's a ladies room hiding in the woods is there?"

Drake chuckled. "What you see is what you get. Feel free to pick a tree."

"Okay," Cyndi said and trotted into the woods looking as happy as Tigger bouncing through the Hundred Acre Woods.

Drake's eyes trailed to Maggie. "That isn't a problem for you is it?"

She sighed and answered, "Not at all. I packed my T.P."

"You remembered toilet paper but forgot to bring food? Figures," Drake huffed as he set down his backpack.

"Figures? Oh, I get it. Since I don't want to use a leaf I'm automatically out of the survivor of the month club?"

Drake let out a short, humorless laugh. He gathered some twigs and knelt by the fire-pit before saying, "No. You're out because you left any common sense you may have had back in the city." He began placing the twigs in the center of the fire-pit.

Maggie stood indignantly. "Do you go out of your way to offend your guests, Mr. Strong?"

"Only the ones who deserve it."

Maggie looked around for something to throw at him. "And why do I deserve it?"

Drake stood to face her and ran a hand through his hair. "Look. You're out of your element here, and we both know it."

She let the words sink in. "I know," she spoke softly as she admitted the truth. "It was my ex-fiancé's idea of coming here in the first place."

"Then why did you come without him?"

"Because I thought that this would be the last place he would think to look for me."

Surprise registered across his face before he quickly masked it. He crossed his arms over his chest and shook his head. "I knew the first moment I saw you that you were going to be trouble."

Drake turned and walked to the side of the L-shaped building and picked up several pieces of firewood. He came back, knelt down and carefully placed them beside the fire-pit. He glanced up at her and asked, "Why do you need to hide from him?"

Maggie answered with a question of her own, "Why are you hiding?"

A muscle in his jaw twitched before he began arranging the wood in the fire-pit. "I'm not hiding," he grumbled.

Cyndi erupted from behind a tree with more energy than nature should allow, and Dillon came crashing through the woods in the opposite direction. They met in the middle of the camp and joined hands.

Dillon said, "You should have seen the snake I almost stepped on. It was huge."

Maggie looked at Dillon as panic surged through

her, and she jumped up on the picnic table, raising her legs high off the ground.

"Snake? Where?" She scanned the area for signs of the slithery creature.

"Back in the woods." Dillon pointed behind him. "He's probably long gone by now."

Cyndi asked as she pointed across the clearing, "Hey. Where does that trail lead to?" Apparently, the idea of a snake nearby hadn't fazed Cyndi at all.

Drake answered, "It leads to a waterfall about a quarter of a mile away."

"Oh goodie. Let's go Dillon!" she exclaimed as she tugged on his arm.

"Afraid of snakes?" Drake asked as he looked at Maggie when she continued to stay scrunched up on top of the picnic table.

Her face warmed with embarrassment, and she slowly let her legs drop to the ground but continued to keep an eye out for the unwelcome visitor.

"Nothing wrong with being cautious," Maggie defended herself. She watched Cyndi and Dillon disappear down the path. As the area became quiet again, she looked at Drake and asked, "Don't you get lonely out here?"

He finished arranging the logs, dusted his hands and stood up to face her again. A flicker of the truth passed through his eyes before they became guarded. He shrugged his shoulders and replied, "God provides me with what I need."

Maggie nodded her head and chewed on her lower lip. "How long have you lived out here?"

"Two years since the resort opened, and one year before that when I was setting the place up."

"Are you worried you may miss something by being so isolated out here?"

"No. I've seen more of the world than I ever intended to. Besides, I feel more at home here than anywhere else. How about you? Why did you insist on coming here? I'm sure you could have found somewhere else to hide from your fiancé."

Maggie looked away into the forest of trees. "No, I couldn't. He has money, connections. If he decides he wants to find me. He will. Even way out here." Her eyes trailed back to Drake. "This was my best option at the time."

His eyes narrowed. "Why would he follow you? What did you do to him?"

Maggie shrunk inwardly, but maintained an aloof appearance. She held her head high and huffed, "What makes you think I did anything?"

He shrugged his shoulders. "Just a hunch."

"Well your hunch is wrong, Mr. Strong. I'm going to the waterfall," she said dismissively as she started to walk away.

Drake barked, "No you're not."

Maggie stopped and faced him. "Why not?"

"You can't go anywhere alone, remember?"

"But it's only a quarter of a mile away. You said so yourself."

He gave a wry smile. "Knowing you, you'd get yourself lost, cornered by a bear or bitten by a snake." His smile disappeared. "I'm not kidding, Maggie. You will not go anywhere alone. Understood?"

Maggie swallowed against the steely determination radiating from his eyes. She tilted her head and said, "I see you have just about as much confidence in me as I do in myself." She felt tears spring to her eyes and turned away from his probing stare.

****

Drake stood behind Maggie, staring at her back. He watched as she rifled through her backpack. Probably to keep her hands busy, more than anything. He saw her shoulder hitch one time.

"Don't go crying on me now." His words came out gruffer than he intended. He hated seeing a woman cry, especially if it was because of him. His anger deflated, and he felt a touch of compassion strike him. At least she had been honest enough to admit she was out of her element.

When she remained silent he walked up behind her and said, "Many of my guests feel out of place here."

"Actually, I feel more comfortable here than I did back where I came from. Much more comfortable."

Drake raised his eyebrows. "You do?"

"Yeah." Maggie turned to face him. "I didn't fit into my fiancé's world at all. I always felt like I was on the outside looking in. His life was stifling. Here?" She looked around and took in a deep breath. "I feel like I can breathe again."

Drake caught himself before reaching up to pull a strand of hair from her eyes. He didn't want to know anymore than he needed to about this woman. And he certainly didn't need to be touching her. He took a deep breath and guarded his heart saying, "Let's get dinner started."

He watched as she nodded her head. She looked almost as relieved as he felt at the change of subject.

Drake walked over to the storage building and lifted a large rock that sat beside it. He removed a key from under it and unlocked the door to the building.

"It's not much, but it works as a shelter when it's needed."

He led Maggie past several shelves lined with food, emergency equipment and supplies. He continued walking to the end of the narrow passageway and turned left. He stood in the square room that served as his living quarters when he chose to stay here. He flipped on an overhead light and heard Maggie let out a gasp.

"This place has electricity?"

"Sure. Otherwise the refrigerator wouldn't work."

"You have a refrigerator in here?"

Drake gave a reluctant smile and his tense stance relaxed a little. "Right over there." He pointed to the small unit against the far wall. "Next to the microwave."

"What's in there?" She pointed to a narrow door.

"It's an extra supply closet. I keep things like snakebite kits, bandages and other emergency type medications in there." He opened the door to show her.

Maggie took a step toward him. She brushed his arm with hers and jerked back as if he'd shocked her.

Drake looked down into her wide eyes. His voice came out raspy and low as he said, "I know I can be uncivilized at times. But I won't hurt you."

She stood close enough for him to catch a slight wisp of cinnamon radiating from her.

He watched her bite her lower lip and nod before looking away. She looked so vulnerable at that moment, so fragile. He had to remind himself that this woman could stand on her own. She had proven that to him when she refused to let him intimidate her at the check-in center. He thought back to her comment about not having confidence in herself. He meant what he'd said when he told her she had too much pride or not enough confidence, but as he replayed the scene in his head, guilt tugged at him at the harsh way he pointed it out to her.

Drake shut the closet door and started to gather the supplies for dinner. He decided he would try to control his tenuous temper with Maggie. When his guests needed something, he always made sure he provided it, even if it wasn't tangible. He decided he would help her find what she had come out here looking for, even if she didn't know what that something was yet. That way he could keep his conscience free and clear from any guilt when it was time for her to leave.

"Have you stayed up here for long periods of time?" Her question shook him out of his thoughts.

He opened the refrigerator door and nodded. "Last winter I got snowed in for three weeks. Then, after the snow melted, I stayed for another three."

"Why did you stay?"

"Why not? I have what I need here."

"It still sounds lonely to me."

"Are you sure you're not the one who's lonely?" Drake asked as he handed her a package of hot dogs.

Maggie looked down past the package in her hands, as if looking right through it. She lifted her eyes to his and said, "I know I am."

Drake's insides churned at her admittance. "How can you be lonely so quickly? Didn't you just break up with your fiancé a few days ago?"

"Yeah." Her voice came out in a hoarse whisper. "But I've been lonely for much longer than that."

He hesitated. Maggie had a way of bringing forth his well hidden protective instincts. He caught himself wanting to comfort her, but instead of falling into that trap, he straightened his shoulders and asked, "Then that proves you don't have to be isolated to be lonely, doesn't it?"

"Yeah, I guess it does." She suddenly turned and swept around him saying, "I'll get these ready to cook." She held up the hot dogs as she disappeared around the corner.

Drake gathered the buns and condiments, a bag of chips and a few sodas. He left the confines of the storage building and stepped out to find a surprise waiting for him.

Chapter Six

Maggie stood back from the blast of heat as the newly lit fire crackled to life and sparks shot high into the air. The smoke came barreling from the wood in thick waves, choking the tree branches that hung overhead. She warmed her hands as dusk settled in and the temperature dropped a few degrees.

She looked past the fire when Drake emerged from the storage building. She saw the startled look on his face and adrenaline surged through her. She suddenly wondered with a lurch in her stomach if there was a reason she shouldn't have lit the fire.

Drake's face softened and a shadow of a smile appeared on his lips. She saw him sweep his eyes over her before settling them back on her face. He stood, staring at her for a long moment with a package of hot dog buns and a bag of chips squeezed to his chest, sodas in the crook of his arms, and ketchup and mustard bottles hanging precariously from his fingers.

Maggie jumped into action when she realized she had left him to carry the rest of the food. She quickly grabbed the condiments just before he lost his grip on them.

"I'm sorry. I didn't mean to leave you with..." she began to apologize before he cut her off.

"You started the fire on your own?"

"Yeah," Maggie replied. When she saw the question in his eyes she added, "Apparently, I have some hidden abilities."

"Apparently. How did you light it?"

"With my lighter." Maggie pulled out her Zippo

and flicked it open.

"I didn't know you smoke."

"I don't," she said as she carried the dinner items to the table. "My father taught me to carry one with me when I was growing up. He told me to always expect the unexpected and be prepared." She laughed softly and shrugged her shoulders. "At least I came prepared for something right?"

Drake's small smile turned into a larger one. His dimple appeared and his even, white teeth showed his amusement in the dimming light. "What else do you have hidden in that bag of yours?"

"A hairbrush, toothbrush, rubber bands, toothpicks, cell phone, romance novel, clothes detergent, you know, the usual."

Drake ambled over and set the sodas, chips and bread down on the table. One of the sodas rolled to the ground before he could catch it. After swooping the can up from the ground, he pretended to lean over and peek in her bag.

"Rubber bands, clothes detergent, toothpicks?"

"You never know."

"Cell phones don't work out here."

"Even from the top of the mountains?"

"Not anywhere out here."

"I didn't think so. But I feel naked without it." Maggie immediately wished she had chosen different words as she felt another embarrassing blush rise up her cheeks.

Drake's eyes darkened for a moment before he looked down at the soda he still held in his hands. He fumbled with the tab on top then popped it open. Fizz spewed out from the top, drenching his hands and landing on his boots.

Maggie leapt back and laughed. Drake looked perplexed for a fraction of a second until he realized what he had done.

Maggie asked, "Forgot you dropped it?"

Drake set it down and picked up another soda

can. He looked at Maggie with a mischievous grin and began to shake it. He took one step toward her, then another.

She looked down at the can and shook her head saying, "Oh, no you don't." She turned on her heel and ran as fast as she could, but Drake ran past her and blocked her path.

He quirked his eyebrows at her and stood poised and ready to open it on her. "You dare laugh at me?" His grin betrayed his menacing words.

Maggie held her hands up in defense and shouted, "With you! I'm laughing with you." She couldn't hold back another giggle as he teased her again with the shaken soda can.

Cyndi and Dillon came striding up into camp. Immediately sobered, Drake let the can drop to his side.

He walked up beside Maggie and leaned in whispering, "You are one lucky lady."

His breath skimmed her ear, slid down her neck and jolted her senses. She drew in a quick breath as she watched him walk away.

Cyndi walked over to her and said, "You should see the waterfall, it's amazing!"

Maggie drew her eyes from Drake and smiled at Cyndi. "I would like to."

Drake asked, "Is anyone hungry?"

Cyndi, Dillon and Maggie all answered at the same time, "I am!"

"Then let's eat." Drake went to the storage building and pulled out folding camping chairs and set them around the fire. Each of them took a seat and took turns cooking their own hot dogs. The smell of the burning wood combined with the juicy hot dogs sent Maggie's stomach roiling and rumbling.

"I don't usually drool over hot dogs. But these smell so good," Maggie admitted.

"Mmm. They are." Cyndi stuffed her cheeks full as she looked at Dillon. He nodded and grinned as he ate.

Maggie wrapped one in a bun and took a bite of the best hot dog she had ever tasted. She closed her eyes and chewed, enjoying the earthy flavor of her meal.

"I didn't peg you for a fan of hot dogs," Drake said, breaking through her moment.

Maggie opened her eyes and found Drake studying her with curiosity as he bit into his second hot dog.

"You seem to have a lot of pre-conceived notions about me. What exactly did you peg me as liking?"

He ran his eyes over her. "Lobster. Caviar."

Maggie shuddered. "Ick. Try again." She challenged as she took another bite.

"Salads and tofu?"

Maggie smiled and laughed. "Try steaks and potatoes. Pizza and beer."

Cyndi chimed in, "Chocolate cake."

"Oh, definitely chocolate cake. And chocolate chip cookies, pastries...muffins. Apple pies."

Drake commented, "You sound like a junk food addict."

"Not really. I don't eat that much of what I bake. If I did it would cut into my profits too much. Not to mention my waistline."

Drake took a swig of soda. "Profits?"

"I'm a baker. I had a bakery back in L.A."

Maggie watched Drake's curiosity spark once again. He lifted his eyebrows and nodded as he reached for a bag of chips and asked, "Is that where you're from?"

"No. I grew up in Texas."

"How did you end up in California?"

"I wanted to try something different. Go somewhere new. I have four overprotective brothers that like to try to run my life. I needed to know I could make it on my own. So I tried it."

Dillon asked, "You said you had a bakery? What

happened to it?"

Maggie forced herself to look at Dillon. "I closed it."

Cyndi said, "You weren't making enough money?"

"I made plenty of money. I closed it for personal reasons."

"Did your ex have anything to do with that?" Cyndi probed.

Maggie nodded. "Yep." She took another bite of her hot dog and, becoming uncomfortable, quickly changed the subject. "I could go for some smores tonight."

"We can make those," Drake said as he stood. He finished his second hotdog and threw his napkin into the fire. "I have the graham crackers, marshmallows and chocolate. I'll get them."

When Drake disappeared inside the building, Cyndi popped up and came over to Maggie. "He's got the ingredients for smores on hand? He's my hero. What do you think?" She playfully nudged Maggie in the arm.

"I think he doesn't like me."

"Naw..."

"He nearly attacked me on the trail for not asking him to slow down. Cyndi, he doesn't think I belong out here."

"Did he tell you that?"

"He used different words...but yeah he did."

"Bummer," Cyndi sighed.

"I'm not looking anyway, remember?"

"Can't blame me for trying can you?"

Maggie smiled. "No. I think Aunt Cammie is trying too."

Drake came out with the makings for the smores, and Cyndi flounced back to sit next to her husband.

Dillon asked, "So where do we sleep?"

"In tents. I'll bring them out after we put away

the food. We should cook the smores and put away the leftovers. Last time I brought a group up here we had a bear visit us."

Cyndi asked, "While you were eating dinner?"

"No. One of the couples decided to have a late night snack inside their tent, against my advice of course, and the bear went after it."

Maggie's heart lurched. "What happened?"

"The bear got what he wanted."

"Was anyone hurt?"

"No. Luckily the couple escaped from the tent before the bear tore it to shreds. I'll never forget it. It was around two in the morning when I first smelled the bear."

"What does a bear smell like?" Cyndi interrupted.

Drake looked at Cyndi and answered, "You'll know if one is nearby. It's hard to explain. They have their own unique, wild animal smell. I recognized it and when I got up, I found a black bear beside one of the couple's tents. I tried to warn them, but apparently they knew it was there because they came scrambling out. They were both completely naked." Drake chuckled and gave a wide, attention-getting smile.

"Oh how embarrassing," Maggie commented.

"They didn't even realize they were nude until after the bear had left. They were too busy trying to climb up a tree to get away from it."

Maggie couldn't help but to smile at the image Drake portrayed. Then she asked, "Can you get away from a bear by climbing a tree?"

"Not usually. Bears can climb better and higher than most people," Drake answered then pointed to some nearby trees. "See those lines in the trees where the bark has been torn off?"

Maggie looked at the tree trunks. She saw the bare wood underneath what looked like long scratch marks in the bark. Some of them reached high into the air. "I see them."

"Those are from bears climbing the trees to play."

"To play?"

Drake nodded then a smile broke out on his face. "Unless they were after some unfortunate hiker that thought he could climb up a tree to get away."

"Were the people in the tent ever in real danger?" Cyndi asked.

Drake nodded. "Some bears can be very aggressive. So yes, they were in danger. I'd have to say they learned their lesson from the experience."

Cyndi said, "Well, let's get the smores cooked so we can put away the food. I don't want to be running naked from a bear tonight."

Everyone agreed and set about making their treats. It didn't take long for each of them to have their fill of the sugary snack and Drake and Dillon quickly stored away all of the remaining food.

Cyndi started yawning and said, "We should set up our tents."

Drake and Dillon broke out of their conversation and headed to the building to gather the supplies. Drake came back with two tents and gave one to Dillon and Cyndi. He headed toward Maggie with the other one.

"Are you going to sleep inside the storage building?" Maggie asked, suddenly nervous at the thought of being outside without him. The knowledge that she wanted him close by for protection unsettled her. She didn't think it wise to start thinking of him as anything other than her host.

"No. I'm sleeping under the stars tonight."

Maggie's eyes widened. "Really? Won't the snakes crawl into your sleeping bag?"

"I sure hope not," Drake answered with a laugh.

"How many times have you slept outside?"

"I don't know...more than I can count. I spent

months in the jungle on various deployments when I was a SEAL. I'm used to it. Having a sleeping bag is a luxury," he said and started helping Maggie set up her tent. "Do you want to try it?"

"No thanks," she said shaking her head quickly. "I prefer to have something between me and the bugs." After she said it, she wondered briefly what it would be like. She might just have the nerve to try it if Drake were there beside her. Her breathing hitched at the turn her thoughts had taken. She picked up a folded tent pole and snapped the lengths together trying to redirect her thoughts. She reached for another and pain shot through one of her fingers as she grabbed for it. She jerked back and saw she had cracked a nail.

"You okay?" Drake asked as he continued to set up her tent.

"Yeah. I just broke a nail," Maggie replied. She tried to continue helping set up the tent but her nail kept getting snagged on the material. Frustrated, she reached for her backpack and dug out a pair of nail clippers. She began snipping her manicured nails off, one by one until she noticed Drake looking at her as if she had just landed on earth from another planet.

"What?" She stopped in mid-snip.

He raised his eyebrows. "You're cutting your nails?"

"Yeah." Maggie looked down and continued to snip. "Why?"

"I'm just surprised that's all."

"I broke one. Now I have a reason to get rid of all of them," she looked back into his questioning eyes.

Drake looked more confused than ever. "You don't like them long?"

"Not really. My ex-fiancé was the one who insisted I keep them this way. It actually feels really good to get rid of them." She smiled and snapped off the last one with gusto.

"What else did he insist you do?"

Maggie busied herself by putting the clippers away. "Lots of things." Admitting it out loud proved to be harder than admitting it to only herself. Embarrassed, she looked away from Drake and noticed that Cyndi and Dillon had finished setting up their tent and had gone inside already.

Drake brought her attention back to him when he asked, "Did you always do what he asked?"

"Almost always," she reluctantly admitted.

Drake shook his head and finished setting up the tent.

Maggie stiffened. "What are you thinking?"

"I'm thinking," he paused as he stood back and studied the position of the tent, "That you're lucky you didn't marry him." He moved the tent a foot to the side, hammered the tent stakes into the ground and said, "You should be good to go. I'll get a sleeping bag for you." He briskly walked to the storage building.

Maggie stared at Drake's back and knew he was right, and he didn't even know the worst part of it.

Chapter Seven

"Cyndi and Dillon will ride down first," Drake explained the next morning as they made their way down the trail leading to the zip line ride. "Then I'll ride down with Maggie."

Cyndi squealed. "It's a tandem ride? Oh, I can't wait. Dillon, we get to ride together!"

Dillon answered with a bright smile.

Maggie trudged along behind them. She had been quiet this morning as they had put away the tents and eaten breakfast. Drake could tell by the way Maggie had moved around so stiffly when she woke, that she felt the strain of yesterday's hike in her calve muscles, and probably many other places as well. He had seen her dig around in her backpack for a couple of pain pills, but he hadn't heard one complaint from her.

He kept his pace slow, telling himself it was because they weren't in a hurry, but deep down he knew he did it to give Maggie an easier time. He glanced back at her and immediately noticed a new anxiety, both in her eyes and in the way she nipped on her bottom lip with her teeth. His breath caught in his chest as he wondered what it would be like to feel those lips pressed against his. He snapped his head back around, chastising himself for thinking of Maggie as a woman, and not just his guest. He kept his eyes straight ahead for the remainder of the walk, and tried to keep the image of Maggie's lips far from his mind.

When they came around a bend in the trail, the launch tower for the zip line ride came into view. Cyndi and Dillon ran past Drake and climbed up the tower. He turned to check on Maggie. She had stopped and stood looking at him like he had just led her to the gallows. Her face had paled and her eyes had widened. She looked more frightened now than she had before stepping into the seaplane.

His heart squeezed in his chest. He cleared his throat before saying, "Let's go on up, and I'll explain how this works."

Once they had all climbed the tower, Drake let them take in the view for a few minutes.

"It's beautiful," Maggie exclaimed, as she held on to the railing with white-knuckled intensity.

Drake came to stand beside her as he looked out at the vast wilderness that spread out before them. The mountain ranges multiplied in the distance, creating an unending view of mountain tops and valleys, hills and slopes. The cable ran high above the tree tops and down toward the valley as far as they could see. His anticipation grew, as it always did, before gliding down the length of the cable. The view never failed to take his breath away. But this time promised to be different. He had always glided alone, this time he would have Maggie with him.

He turned to study her and saw the fear in her eyes melt away as she scanned the horizon. Until she looked down.

He saw the moment the fear jolted back into her. Her breathing hitched and her eyes widened. He had seen the same type of fear in his other guests eyes, and some had even opted to walk down the trail instead of riding the zip line, but he knew in his gut Maggie wouldn't back down from a challenge.

"This ride has been professionally installed by the company that produces the zip line trolley. It's been inspected by an engineering firm, and I assure you it is safe." He pointed to the trolley that held the harness to the cable and explained, "The wheel is encased inside the trolley system, there's no way for it to jump off the cable. It also encompasses a braking system to keep the rate of decent controlled. The lanyard will be attached, as an extra measure of safety." Drake took hold of the tandem harness outfit and said, "Once I get you settled into the straps, you'll line up behind the safety gate. When you're ready to go, I'll open the gate and you'll be on your way."

He saw Maggie shove her hands into the pockets of her well-fitting jeans as she commented, "That's a long way down if this wire pops."

"It won't." Drake tried to assure her, but he had a feeling nothing short of experiencing the ride for herself would dissuade her fears.

Cyndi and Dillon stepped into the harnesses, and Drake secured the lines. They were ready to go in no time. "Once you get to the bottom, attach the trolley to the retrieval system and send it back up. No need to wait for us. Once it's on its way back up the mountain, you two go ahead and follow the trail back to the cabins."

They readily agreed. Drake opened the gate and they sped away, zipping down the slope.

Drake turned to Maggie and smiled. "You okay?"

She nodded and his heart skipped a beat when she pulled at her bottom lip again with her teeth. He looked away again quickly before his mind took him where it didn't belong.

They waited in silence for the trolley to return. When it finally did, he took hold of the harness and asked, "So how does a gutsy woman like you end up afraid of so many things?"

Maggie turned her head a few degrees to acknowledge his question. "I wouldn't call myself gutsy, and I'm not afraid of that many things."

Drake let out a small chuckle as he helped her step into the harness. "No? How about the airplane ride?"

"Any person with common sense would be uneasy riding in one of those tiny things."

"What about snakes?"

"Everyone is afraid of snakes."

"Not everyone."

"Well, everyone should be."

"Okay, fair enough. How about this zip line? Are you afraid of heights too?" He continued questioning her as he stepped into the harness behind her.

"No. I'm just afraid of falling. Look at that tiny wire that's holding us up."

"That tiny wire you're referring to is a three-quarter of an inch diameter steel wire cable. It'll hold somewhere around 69,000 pounds. You have nothing to worry about," Drake reassured her.

"How old is the wire?"

"It's a cable and it's been here for two years. I'll replace it in another two," Drake said as he put a hand on her shoulder and added in a serious tone, "I wouldn't put you or any of my guests in danger. You don't need to worry."

"My fears aren't always rational," Maggie admitted softly.

Drake heard the break in her voice but pressed on. "You opened up your own bakery in unfamiliar surroundings without any help from family or friends. That takes a lot of nerve. What happened to the fearless woman who did that?"

Maggie turned back to face the canopy of trees in front of them. Her hair, silky and smelling of spiced apples and fresh cinnamon, brushed his chin. Drake had meant to get her mind off of her fears, but so far had only succeeded in distracting himself. Her soft, feminine form didn't go unnoticed as he tightened the straps, securing her close to the length of him.

"Nathan happened."

"Who's Nathan? The runaway husband of yours?"

"He's not my husband. But he's the one who was supposed to be."

"What did he do to you to make you so afraid? Did he abuse you?" Drake stiffened, surprised at the turn his own thoughts had taken him. He waited, unmoving for her reply.

"Not physically," she began speaking and ran through the words quickly. "In a nutshell, Nathan came barreling into my life, offered me everything I had hoped and dreamed for and I took the bait. I followed him, blindly. I gave up what I had worked so hard for, and I lost myself somewhere along the way."

"You lost yourself? Is that what you meant last night when you said you almost always did what he wanted you to do?" Drake prompted as he adjusted his harness.

"Yeah. He convinced me to sell my bakery, give up my apartment and move to his parent's mansion until the wedding. It all made sense at the time, but looking back I can see what a mistake I made. I gave up my life and my identity to please him."

"So, that's how he stripped you of your confidence?"

He felt, rather than heard her sharp intake of breath. It took her a moment to respond but when she did, she spoke so low he could barely make out the words.

"No. It happened when he showed me I wasn't good enough, no matter what I did to please him."

"Good enough?" Drake asked as he double-checked the safety lanyard.

"I caught him in bed with another woman."

Drake heard the pain come right through her voice. He stopped moving and said, "That explains why he's not here."

"Yep."

"So, let me get this straight. This guy comes in, takes over your life by offering you the moon and stars, cheats on you and leaves you homeless, jobless and without a shred of self confidence."

"That about sums it up. Except I was the one who left. He still wanted to go through with it. He was furious when I refused to marry him."

"Did he threaten you?"

"Not directly. But from what I saw of his temper, I knew he was capable of hurting me."

"Did you come here looking for more than a hiding place?"

Maggie shrugged but didn't answer. If the question took her by surprise, she didn't show it.

"Well, if you came here looking to restore your shattered confidence you came looking in the wrong place," he said as he finished tightening the straps.

"I never thought of it that way. I came to decide what to do with the rest of my life."

"And?"

"And I haven't had time to figure it out yet."

"Have you prayed about it?"

Her head whipped around sharply, he could see the surprise in her profile. "Some."

"What you're looking for can't be found within yourself or anybody else. If you trust in the Lord with all your heart and ask him to lead you, you won't have to worry about taking the wrong path again. He'll be directing you."

"So you think I'm worried about taking the wrong path?"

"What else? You can open up another bakery. You can live anywhere you want. But you don't know which way to go, do you?"

"No."

"And you don't have the confidence in yourself to make that decision?"

She shook her head, sending another tempting wave of cinnamon his way.

"Not anymore, no."

"Then, you came looking to get some of your confidence back, right?"

"I guess so. Do you analyze all of your guests

this way?"

"No. But, then again," Drake began as he slung his backpack on one shoulder and Maggie's backpack on his other shoulder, "I've never had to look after a stray before. Everyone else comes readymade with a partner."

Drake knew he had accomplished his mission in distracting her when he she stiffened and threw an elbow into his gut.

"Oooff! What was that for?"

"You know what that was for Mr. Strong."

"So we've reverted to Mr. Strong again? I thought we had gotten past the formalities."

"Yeah, well that's before you insulted me."

Drake took a step closer to the edge, ready to use her anger as a way to help her past her fear.

Maggie stiffened and turned her wide eyes to him. "Wait!" Her fingers turned into claws as she grasped for his arm.

"I sure am glad you cut your nails. Relax. I told you I wouldn't go until you said you were ready."

"I know, but you took a step forward. And we're so close to the edge." She turned forward and peeked down. "Okay. So maybe I am afraid of heights."

"The safety gate is still closed, Maggie. It's your choice of when to open it. And until then, there's no way we can get past it."

"Sorry. I'm just a scaredy-cat."

"What's it gonna take for you to trust me?"

"I don't trust myself, how am I supposed to trust anyone else?"

Drake stood steady and dropped his head down until his lips came close to her ear. "One step at a time." He put his hands on her shoulders and said, "The first step is yours to take. Open the gate."

****

Maggie's goose bumps traveled from her neck all the way down her arms and legs.

She swallowed hard. "Is everything ready? I

mean, is it all secured? All of the strap thingies?"

A low, deep chuckle erupted from Drake. "You mean the harnesses? Yes. You're safe."

"Then why don't I feel like it?"

"Have you felt safe since you found Nathan cheating on you?"

Maggie didn't have to think long to have the answer to that question. "No." She shook her head. "I haven't."

"Then the tiny wire and strap thingies, as you call them, aren't your problem are they?"

Maggie shook her head. "No. I guess not." She looked down at the gate. She hugged her arms and took a deep, shaky breath and asked, "Will you put your arms around me?" She felt Drake's muscles tense as she waited for an answer. She swallowed down her fear that he would refuse her.

After a moment, he slid his hands off of her shoulders and wrapped his arms around her. Maggie immediately felt safer as she took refuge in his warm strength.

"Feel better?" His low voice rasped in her ear.

Maggie nodded.

"Good. Are you ready?"

She nodded again and lifted the latch on the gate with trembling fingers. She stood for a moment paralyzed. She thought Drake would have them flying down the mountain by now. But he stood still, waiting.

"Tell me," he said.

With those two words, she began to trust him. He had kept his word. He waited for her to make the decision, just like he said he would.

"Now." Maggie nearly choked on the word and closed her eyes. *Please God, keep us safe!*

"Lift your feet."

Maggie did. She sat suspended for a fraction of a second, until Drake lifted his feet off of the platform. Then, her stomach dropped as they began their decent down the mountain. She turned her head and tucked it into his shoulder as wind blasted her face. The trolley made a zipping sound as they sped along the cable.

"Open your eyes, Maggie."

She peeked out of one eye, before opening both of them. The breathtaking view flew past them. Her fear turned into admiration as she saw the tops of the trees whiz past underneath her feet and as she viewed the mountain ranges in the distance. She began to feel a sense of unmatched freedom as the rushing air cooled her and Drake's arms kept her feeling secure.

A smile spread across her face and she laughed. "This is great!" she yelled back at Drake. Then she stiffened as the acceptor tower came into view at the end of the line. "Aren't we going a little bit fast to stop on that little platform?"

"Trust me."

She held her breath as they came to the end. As they slid nearer and nearer, her newfound sense of freedom gave way to a growing unease. Then the unease turned into deep-rooted fear.

"It's okay, Maggie." Drake's voice held a confidence she wished she felt.

They came to the platform and rolled into a sudden, swinging stop. It hadn't turned out so bad after all. Maggie smiled in relief.

Drake unfastened the harnesses. When free of the straps, she turned to face him and jumped at him, flinging her arms around his neck.

"That was awesome!" she exclaimed as she clung to him.

Drake kept his arms to his sides. He stood as still and as solid as a granite wall. It took a moment to register, but Maggie soon realized what she had done and that she still dangled from Drake Strong's rigid neck.

She let go, and felt her face heat with

embarrassment. "Sorry." She cleared her throat as she looked away from him.

He cleared his throat too and said, "I'm glad you enjoyed the ride." He attached the trolley and harnesses to the retrieval system and sent the equipment back up the mountain toward the loading station. "This'll take a few minutes. Then we'll head back."

The awkward moment lingered and Maggie looked everywhere but at Drake. She studied the hiking trail as it wound its way down the mountain then she studied the trees and plant life. Next, she resorted to shuffling her feet and studying the laces on her boots as if they fascinated her.

"I could kiss you now and get it over with."

Maggie's breath hitched and she felt her face heat to a higher degree. "Excuse me?" She finally met his eyes.

He tilted his head to the side and lifted his shoulders. "To avoid any future awkward moments in case you decide to throw yourself into my arms again."

Maggie's eyes narrowed. "No need. I won't be throwing myself anywhere near you again."

"Are you sure about that?" He asked and took a step closer to her. His lips turned up into a cunning smile.

"Quite sure, Mr. Strong." Maggie turned away and quickly climbed down the steps of the tower.

Chapter Eight

Maggie woke before dawn the next morning from a restless night of broken sleep. She had sore muscles from the hike and confused emotions running through her. She thought about Drake's comment about kissing her and felt an unexpected tingle shoot up her spine as she climbed out of bed. She couldn't help but wonder what it would feel like to be held in his strong arms and feel his lips on hers. A tug of guilt went through her at the thought, but she quickly reminded herself that she had recently become a single woman again with no romantic ties or responsibilities.

She needed to clear her head and get her mind off of Drake's comment, and she knew exactly how to do it. After getting dressed, she headed for the kitchen and baked three kinds of muffins, a pile of cinnamon buns and a peach cobbler. Baking always helped her relax and take her mind off of her circumstances. She had just pulled the cobbler out of the oven when Aunt Cammie made her way into the kitchen to make breakfast.

"Can I help?" Maggie offered cheerfully.

"You already have dear. Mmm. That smells mighty good. Let's have muffins, cinnamon buns and cold cereal this morning. What do you say?"

"Works for me." Maggie looked at Aunt Cammie who still wore her robe and had the signs of sleep adorning her face. She added, "I'm glad you don't mind me using your kitchen."

"Mind? Maggie, if I had my way, you'd be here every day cooking with me."

"Thanks. You make me feel very welcome here."

"You are welcome dear, now that I don't have to cook breakfast, I can go back to bed for half an hour. Oops. I almost forgot. Would you mind fixing up a pot of coffee and taking a cup of it to Drake? I always make sure he gets one in the morning. Otherwise he gets a little grumpy."

"So coffee is the key to keeping him happy? I'll have to remember that." Maggie moved to the pot to start preparing the coffee. Her nerves came to alert at the prospect of going to find Drake this morning, but since Aunt Cammie asked, she would do it.

"Does he like sugar or cream?"

"Neither. He likes it as black as the bears that come to visit us on occasion. Thanks dear," Aunt Cammie said and shuffled back through her door.

"No problem." She wondered what Drake would think of her bringing him coffee. She nervously nibbled on a strawberry muffin while waiting for the coffee to brew. As the deep aroma started filtering into the kitchen, she thought of things to say to him.

They had barely spoken the rest of the way down the mountain yesterday after the zip line ride. She had been too embarrassed from throwing herself at him to even make eye contact. She wondered if she'd still feel awkward when she saw him this morning.

When they had returned yesterday, he'd disappeared inside his cabin without a word. Maggie had noticed Cyndi and Dillon lounging on the dock in each others' arms. A pang of need coursed through her as she remembered how in love the couple seemed to be. Even though she had been dreadfully hurt by Nathan, a part of her still longed for someone to share her life with.

She now understood Nathan had been wrong for her. Even if he hadn't cheated on her, they would have never been right for each other. Her reaction to Drake had proven it beyond a reasonable doubt.

Throughout the whole time she and Nathan had

dated, he had never made her toes tingle or her heart race the way Drake's one comment about kissing her had, even if he didn't really mean it. After all, the man didn't even like her. Maggie sighed and finished the strawberry muffin. She didn't hesitate to pick up a blueberry muffin and start to nibble on it next.

Maggie tried to brush her reaction to him off, but each time she thought of him her pulse quickened and some sort of tingle, quiver or shake attacked her. She had never reacted to a man like she did to Drake, and at the moment, she wasn't too happy about it.

She glanced at the coffee pot, which had finished brewing and started searching for coffee cups. She found a set of mugs and poured two cups. She added cream to one and took a sip as she picked up the other and headed out the door.

The clear skies and bright, crisp air refreshed Maggie as she stepped outside and headed for Drake's cabin. As she walked, she tried to steady her nerves and swallow her anticipation about seeing him again.

She stepped up on his porch, set the mugs down on the railing and raised her hand to the door, but before she could knock she heard Drake call out from behind the cabin. "Back here."

She picked up the mugs and headed around back, taking another sip of caffeine to fortify her to be in Drake's company once again. As she rounded the corner, she nearly bumped into him, sending a few drops of the coffee sloshing to the ground and knocking her off balance.

Drake immediately reached out and grabbed her arms to help steady her. "Whoa. Are you in a hurry?"

"No. I just didn't see you there. I brought some coffee for you."

Drake released her arms, took the cup and mumbled, "Thanks." He took a sip and studied her.

"Give it a few days. You'll unwind and learn how to relax."

Maggie straightened her spine. "I am relaxed." *Thanks to the muffins, cinnamon buns and peach cobbler*, she thought to herself.

"Really? Then I'd hate to see you stressed out."

Maggie sighed, "Good morning to you too."

He chuckled and set the cup down. He turned to face a set of canoes sitting on racks behind him. He started tugging on ropes and tying knots.

Maggie refused to let him rattle her so she ignored his comments about her being in a hurry and tense. "I didn't know you have canoes. Why don't you have them out for us to use?"

"I put them away the first weekend in September. The lake water gets too cold for swimming, and I don't want anyone to fall in by accident."

"That's too bad, I'd love to take a canoe out."

"It's too dangerous. If you fell in, the cold water would take your breath away and make it hard to swim."

"What else do you put away in the fall?"

"I have a set of kayaks." He pointed further into the woods. "I have a paddle boat too, but I had to take it in for repairs because it sprang a leak this past summer."

"I bet it's fun here in the summer."

"Each season has its own advantages. It won't be too long before the leaves start changing. It's a beautiful sight."

"I can imagine. It must be nice to live here."

Drake shot a disbelieving look at her. "I can't imagine someone like you being happy here for long."

"What do you mean someone like me?" This time Maggie's defenses rose quickly. All thoughts of keeping him from rattling her flew away.

He shrugged. "You admitted you're out of your

element here. After all, there's no shopping mall or theater in the woods. You'd get bored."

"I'm not so sure about that."

He stopped working with the ropes and let his eyes roam over her. "Just because you clipped your manicured nails and stopped wearing too much makeup doesn't mean you belong out here."

Maggie bit her cheek to keep from saying something unfiltered as the hurt washed over her. She watched him for a moment and took a sip of coffee to delay her reaction to him. He couldn't know how much she wanted and needed to belong, so she knew he hadn't meant to hurt her. But it did hurt, just the same.

She thought about his comment about wearing too much makeup. She hadn't realized it, but now that he mentioned it, she had stopped worrying as much about lipstick, blush and mascara. Without Nathan around, she didn't feel the need to appear flawless.

She had never belonged in Nathan's world, at his country club or at the yacht parties. She never could golf worth anything and had embarrassed herself completely on the tennis court to the point where Nathan had refused to take her again. Drake's resort had to be the farthest from Nathan's high society life, and if she didn't belong in a place like this either, where did she belong?

Drake continued to stare at her and she finally admitted, "Right now, I don't know where I belong." She turned from him before he saw how much his words had truly affected her. She walked away, shaken by his honesty. She didn't know why his opinion mattered so much to her, but it did, and right now it hurt.

By the time Maggie made her way back to the kitchen, she had mulled over Drake's words. She realized his comment had hurt so much because not only did she want to belong, she had wanted him to accept her being here. Apparently, that wasn't going to happen anytime soon, if at all.

Maggie walked back into the kitchen and saw Aunt Cammie near the counter. She had all the cereal out and ready to be taken outside. She had exchanged her robe for regular clothes and looked much more awake than she did earlier.

"Did you find Drake?" Aunt Cammie asked with a bright smile.

"Yes. Let me help you carry the cereal." Maggie grabbed three boxes of cereal and headed outside, she didn't want to explain her conversation with Drake to his aunt, fearful that Aunt Cammie may see the hurt in her eyes. She passed Drake on the way out and tried to avoid looking at him, but he walked right in front of her and stopped.

"Let me take those."

"It's okay. I've got..." Maggie started to say but Drake took the boxes out of her grasp anyway.

He met her eyes. "Go sit and relax. You're a guest remember?"

Maggie started to argue but reminded herself to pick her battles. Some things just weren't worth fighting over. She made her way over to the picnic tables and listened to the conversation going on around her.

Cyndi and Dillon sat huddled together, Stephen and Beverly sat at opposite ends of the table from each other, and Annie and Larry hadn't arrived yet. Maggie watched Drake set the cereal boxes on the picnic table and head back to the kitchen.

Cyndi smiled at Maggie and passed a bowl to her. "The cave trip is coming up in a few days, aren't you exited?" she asked and did a little hop in her seat, right at the table.

Maggie wished she could have stored up some of the energy she had when she was in her twenties; she sure could use it now. "Right now I'm thinking of a long soak in the Jacuzzi."

Stephen looked up, let his eyes roam over her and winked. Beverly saw him but this time she appeared immune to his flirting, and she returned her focus to the muffin in front of her without comment.

Revulsion crept up Maggie's spine. She couldn't let it go this time. "Stephen, do you always disrespect your wife like you just did?"

Beverly shot Maggie a surprised look. For a moment, she wondered if anyone had bothered to defend her before. Beverly gave Maggie a hesitant smile. Stephen huffed and dug into his cereal bowl.

Dillon asked, "How about it Stephen? What gives?"

Stephen looked up with a challenge in his eyes. "What's it to you?"

Dillon looked at Cyndi and asked, "If I looked at Maggie the way Stephen just did, what would you think?"

"I'd die inside."

Dillon nodded at her then looked to Stephen. "Think about what it does to your wife."

Beverly asked, "What makes you think he'd care?" She left the table, abandoning the rest of her breakfast.

Stephen watched her walk away with a hint of remorse in his eyes. "I didn't think…"

"Why don't you go talk to her?" Maggie asked.

He looked at her and nodded. As he rose he mumbled, "I'm sorry to offend you."

Maggie almost fell off of the bench when she heard his words. That was the last thing she had expected him to say. Maybe Stephen wasn't completely hopeless after all.

"Thanks for stepping in Dillon," Maggie said.

He nodded his head in reply.

Cyndi planted a firm kiss on Dillon's mouth before saying, "Aren't I the luckiest girl?"

"You're both lucky."

Having lost her appetite, she picked up after herself, Stephen and Beverly and carried the bowls and leftovers to the kitchen. She elbowed her way in the door and almost ran into Drake as he headed out.

"You just can't sit back and relax can you?" He said as he took some of the load from her and returned to the kitchen.

"Sure I can. As a matter of fact, I plan to be a hermit for the rest of the day."

He lifted his eyebrows then went to the sink and placed the dishes inside. Maggie followed and did the same. When she started to run the water to wash them off, Drake grabbed her wrist.

He said, "You keep that up and Aunt Cammie's going to think you're after her job."

Concern for Drakes' aunt rose suddenly in her heart. "Speaking of Aunt Cammie, I think she needs help sooner than you think. Feeding so many people on her own is too much for her."

Sudden concern etched Drake's features and he let go of her wrist. "We've talked about hiring someone sometime in the future. Why do you think she needs help soon?"

"She told me the other night that her back ached, and when I baked the muffins and cinnamon buns for breakfast, she took the opportunity to go back to bed for a while."

"*You* made the cinnamon buns?"

His question surprised her. "Yeah..." she hesitated. "Why? Is there something wrong with them?" She glanced over her shoulder at the remaining ones that still rested on the counter.

"No," he answered looking at her with an odd expression on his face.

"What is it?"

"Nothing." He shook his head as he turned on the water and started washing the dishes himself.

Maggie picked up a dish towel and chewed on

her lip.

"I wish you'd stop doing that," Drake growled.

"Doing what?" She slapped the dish towel down on the counter, aggravated beyond reason at his strange behavior.

"Biting your lower lip like that. It's too sexy."

The room heated ten degrees, and Maggie felt blood rush to her cheeks. She looked away from him and picked up the dish towel again. "Oh."

Aunt Cammie came through the door from her rooms and beamed a smile at the two of them standing at the counter together. "I should take a break more often." She ambled up to the counter and piled the remaining muffins and cinnamon buns into a storage container. "Drake, you said these cinnamon buns were the best you'd ever tasted. Did you know Maggie baked them?"

He nodded. "Just found out."

Maggie looked at him, suddenly understanding his odd behavior. He didn't want her to know he liked the food she had baked.

Drake cleared his throat and studied the dishes.

Aunt Cammie flitted outside to continue with her job, leaving them in awkward silence.

"Why didn't you tell me you liked my buns?" *Oh dear Lord, did I just say that?*

The look on Drake's face confirmed she had indeed just said that. His lips quirked, his eyes trailed down to her jeans and his blue eyes sparkled.

Her mouth dropped opened and then it closed again. Maggie figured there wasn't a word in the English language that would get her foot out of her mouth at this point.

Drake's face broke out into an enormous grin.

Maggie cleared her throat and said, "I'm just going to take my buns to the cabin and hide-out for a while." She swept past Drake, grabbed a cinnamon bun from the container and headed out the door, mortification followed her every step of the way.

Chapter Nine

Later in the day, Maggie settled into the rocker on the porch with her book in one hand and a cup of tea in the other. She tucked her feet under her and sipped the tea, feeling the relaxing atmosphere seep into her as she finally let the embarrassment from earlier ease. She opened her book to read and immediately became engrossed in the story until a terrified scream echoed across the resort. The lake amplified the sound and it pierced Maggie's ears as if she were right beside the source. She jumped up and dropped her book and the tea cup which shattered at her feet. She ignored the broken porcelain and ran down the porch steps toward the terrified voice.

She counted three separate cries for help as she made her way toward the commotion at the back of Aunt Cammie's Kitchen. When she arrived, she saw Beverly on her knees, crying and nearly hysterical as she leaned over Stephen. He sat on the ground, holding his leg while rocking back and forth. Dillon and Cyndi stood off to the side looking bewildered and Annie stood beside Larry, ringing her hands.

"What happened?"

Dillon looked at Maggie and explained, "He got bitten by a rattler."

Maggie's stomach dropped to her toes. "Are you sure?"

Stephen moaned, "I'm sure. I got a real good look at it as it tore into my leg."

"Stay still Stephen. Stop rocking." Maggie remembered Drake's instructions on restricting movement after a bite.

Aunt Cammie appeared and asked, "What's going on? Why does he need to stay still?"

"Snake bite. Where's Drake? Someone find him!" Maggie yelled. When everyone hesitated she shouted, "Hurry!"

"Oh dear." Aunt Cammie clasped her hands tightly together. "Uh...Maggie?"

Chaos erupted all at once. Annie and Larry scattered away calling for Drake. Dillon knelt down beside Maggie and said, "Stephen, keep your leg below your heart and stay still."

Cyndi started crying and tugging on Dillon. "What if he dies?"

Aunt Cammie said louder, "Maggie!"

She spun her head around. "What is it?"

"Drake's not here. He's gone off. I don't know for how long. Sometimes he's gone for hours."

Maggie's heart lurched. "Can you get in touch with him?"

She shook her head.

Cyndi asked, "Stephen needs help. Call 9-1-1!"

"The road is blocked by the trees! How would they get out here?" Maggie felt dread seep deep into her bones. "Aunt Cammie, call Harley, see if he can bring the seaplane. We could send Stephen to the hospital with him."

Aunt Cammie turned and sped away.

Maggie looked down at Stephen's leg. It had started to swell and it showed signs of discoloration. She prayed, *Lord, help us.* She swallowed the fear down, willing it away. She knew she had to stay calm and think. What would Drake do if he were here? Then she remembered the snakebite kit in the storage building at the top of the eight mile hike.

Aunt Cammie came back wringing her hands. "I can't get a hold of Harley."

"Do you have a snakebite kit close by?"

She shook her head. "I don't know where one is. Drake would know."

"But he's not here," Maggie pointed out. She looked back at Stephen. She saw wild panic in his eyes and noticed his rapid breathing. She put a hand on his wrist and felt his pulse beat quickly beneath her fingers. Sweat beaded on his forehead and ran down his temples.

Stephen turned his wide eyes to her. "Help me." His hoarse voice and pleading words cut into Maggie's heart. She looked down at his wound. Blood oozed from the bite marks and the swelling continued to increase.

"We have to get to the snakebite kit. He needs the anti-venom."

"But we don't know where it is," Cyndi pointed out.

"I know where one is." She glanced between Dillon and Cyndi. "It's up at the overnight camping area inside the storage building. We need it."

Aunt Cammie said, "It'll be getting dark soon. Even if you get there tonight, it'll be morning before you can get back."

"Does anyone have any better suggestions?" Maggie asked.

No one answered and a hush came over the group.

Beverly looked at Maggie with red, swollen eyes. Tears stained her face and her hands shook uncontrollably. "He's all I have. Do something!"

In that instant, Maggie made up her mind. "I'll go up the mountain tonight and head back with the snakebite kit at first light. I need someone to come with me. Drake wouldn't want me to go alone."

"I'll go," Dillon said.

Cyndi grabbed his arm. "But it's getting dark. What if you get lost?"

Dillon answered, "We have to try something, Cyn."

Just then, Stephen rolled to his side and threw up as nausea claimed him.

Beverly screamed again.

Spurred into action, Maggie stood and looked at Dillon. "We need to get him inside."

Dillon agreed and headed toward Stephen. Maggie and Dillon stood on either side of Stephen and hauled him to his cabin.

Once inside Maggie instructed, "Put him in the chair. Keep his leg lowered."

Aunt Cammie came in carrying a bag of frozen peas. "I can't get Harley on the phone. Put these peas on his leg."

Dillon started to take the bag of frozen vegetables.

"No!" Maggie stopped him. "Remember what Drake said. No cold compresses."

"But the swelling..." Aunt Cammie began.

"No. Drake said not to do it. I don't know why. But he said not to."

"Okay," Aunt Cammie relented.

"Dillon, get your backpack. We've got to head up the mountain before it gets too dark."

He nodded his head and left. Maggie turned to follow him out and said, "Cyndi, get Stephen a blanket and a pillow. Make him as comfortable as you can."

Beverly grabbed her arm before she could walk out. "What can I do?" she asked with a shaky voice.

Maggie looked into her wild eyes and answered, "Pray."

Minutes later, Maggie and Dillon started their climb up the mountain. Dillon began to run and Maggie said, "We have to pace ourselves or we'll never make it to the top."

"If it gets too dark we won't be able to see the path. We won't make it to the top that way either. We'll get lost."

"I know."

"Then let's go faster."

Maggie relented and broke into a jog. Her racing

heart doubled its pace as she put unusual demands on it.

They climbed higher and higher, finally Maggie had to stop and catch her breath.

"It's getting too dark," Dillon said as he sucked in deep breaths of air.

Maggie knew by the resigned look in his eyes he had given up even before he said the words.

"I'm going back down."

"You can't leave me alone out here."

"Then come back with me. Maybe Aunt Cammie has gotten a hold of Harley. Maybe Drake has come back."

"And what if she hasn't talked to Harley? What if Drake hasn't come back?"

"Then...I don't know." He swiped beads of perspiration from his brow. "Maggie. I have a wife to think about. I can't go and get myself lost and killed out here. Cyndi needs me."

Maggie didn't want to waste time arguing. "Then you do what you need to do. And I'll do what I need to do."

Dillon glanced up the trail and then back the way they just came. He closed his eyes for a moment before looking at her again. "Take my water. You may need extra."

Maggie's heart sank when she knew he wouldn't change his mind. Panic tried to take hold of her rational thoughts. She stamped down her fears of being alone in the wilderness and took Dillon's canteen. "You'd better head back."

She watched Dillon's retreating back for a moment before she turned to continue her hike. *Alone.* The thought echoed in her head. Drake had warned her not to go anywhere alone. He had warned her to follow his rules. But what choice did she have?

She ignored the persistent warnings deep inside her and kept trekking higher. She stopped occasionally for water and snacked on a granola bar on the way. With each minute that passed the light faded more and her fears deepened.

What if she didn't get there in time? Would she get lost? Would she be forced to sit on the trail all night exposed to the elements and wait for daybreak?

She pushed herself harder as she panted for breath. She recognized a few of the places Drake had pointed out to them on her first trip up here. That comforted her for a few minutes until she no longer recognized any rock formations or trees. As dusk settled in, her fear climbed up into her throat and took her thoughts captive.

Her legs screamed at her, and her heart felt like it would burst. But she had no choice but to push onward. She forced her thoughts to focus on something besides her current circumstances. She wondered what Nathan would have done if he had been here. Would he have come with her up the mountain? She already knew the answer deep in her heart. No, he wouldn't have. Drake's image sprang to mind, and she knew without a doubt that he would do whatever it took to help Stephen.

Maggie heard the night creatures awaken as the sun sank lower. Fear for Stephen pushed her to continue. She heard Beverly's pleas repeat in her head, *he's all I have.* The memories spurred her forward through her mounting fears.

She tried to come up with ways to distract herself. She prayed for a while and then thought about some of her favorite recipes. She recited them in her head to help calm her as the day grew darker and darker. Her strategy worked for a while until panic seized her and she stopped in mid-step. The path had disappeared. She couldn't see the outline of it for a moment and her heart nearly stopped. She looked heavenward and prayed, *Lord, please guide me. Be my light in the darkness of this night...*

She looked around at her feet once again and caught a glimpse of the path. She edged forward a few more steps at a time until she finally came into a clearing. She nearly cried when she recognized the overnight camping area. She had made it to the top. Relief flooded through her, and she sank to her knees. She bent her head and thanked God for keeping her safe.

She sat on her knees for several moments while she caught her breath and tried to temper down her anxiety about Stephen. She knew she had to wait until dawn before she could do anything else for him. She prayed, *Lord, Stephen is in your hands. Please let him be okay.*

It felt strange to sit still and do nothing. She had been reacting on auto-pilot for a few hours now, running on adrenaline alone. As the rush left her, she felt exhaustion settle into her along with an intense hunger. She had missed dinner once again.

She stood slowly on wobbly legs and made her way to the storage building. She remembered where Drake had hidden the key and quickly retrieved it. She slipped inside and walked to the back of the building. When she finally got her hands on the snakebite kit, she felt a sense of accomplishment wash over her. She felt like she had faced a major hurdle and had managed to leap over it.

She found a microwaveable can of soup and popped it into the small microwave to heat. She looked around for a minute while the soup cooked. She suddenly felt like she had intruded on Drake's privacy by coming inside without him, but quickly reminded herself she hadn't had many options available to her. Maggie grabbed the soup when the microwave timer went off and picked up a bag of marshmallows she found on a shelf. Then, she headed outside to build a campfire, hoping it would help to calm her frazzled nerves.

Chapter Ten

Maggie had been settled at the campfire for over an hour when she remembered the bag of marshmallows she brought out with her. She found a suitable stick, impaled a marshmallow on it and held it out over the flames. When a quick moving shadow at the head of the trail caught her eye, the browning marshmallow lost her attention immediately and blood rushed through her veins. Her heart pace increased with sudden fear of the unknown. The fast moving shadow soon developed into a man. Maggie recognized his form before his face came into view. Her racing heart doubled its pace when she knew Drake had come after her. Her immediate relief did a somersault and switched to trepidation when she saw the look of fury on his shadowed features.

Drake stalked toward her like a mountain lion hunting its prey. His breath came in ragged gasps, as if he had run the whole way up the mountain. He came to a sudden stop on the opposite side of the blazing campfire and peeled his backpack from his shoulders. His steely glare pinned her to the ground as he stood beyond the flickering firelight.

"Have you lost your mind?"

Maggie sat frozen under his penetrating gaze until the smell of burning marshmallow brought her focus down from Drake's blue-eyed censure to the stick she still held. The innocent little, white puff of sugar now dangled from the stick, charred and on fire, looking like a drooping torch glowing in the night. She let the stick and ruined marshmallow drop into the burning blaze and prepared herself for

Drake Strong's wrath.

"What did I tell you before I allowed you to come on this retreat?"

"I can explain why…"

"Answer my question," Drake cut off her words.

"You told me not to go anywhere alone."

"And what did you do? Do you have any idea what could have happened to you?" He asked as he threw his hands up in exasperation then rested them on his hips.

"I came after the anti-venom. Stephen was bitten by a rattler and…"

"And you didn't think I had any stored closer than here?" His breathing became more controlled as he watched her and waited for a reply.

"You had some at camp?" Maggie's hope renewed. "Did you give it to him? Is he all right?"

"Yes. He'll be fine. He's already been taken to the hospital."

"How? I thought the road had trees…"

"The road has been cleared since yesterday. Now, answer my question. Did you think I wouldn't have any of the anti-venom at camp?" Drake's impatience showed through his clipped words.

"I figured you would but you weren't there to ask. I had no idea when you'd be back, and no one knew where to look for the medicine. Aunt Cammie didn't even know. What alternative did I have?" Maggie lifted her hands.

Drake slowly walked around the fire with menace in each step. "What alternative did you have? You could have followed my rules."

"I know but, Drake. Listen…" Maggie stood and took a hesitant step backward. "Dillon offered to come with me. And he started to, but when it began to get dark, he bailed out on me. What could I do? A man's life was at stake. I had to try. I had to keep going."

"You should have turned back with him. You put

yourself in danger by disobeying my rules," he said as he stopped walking and pointed a finger at her. "Rules that were made to keep city girls like you out of trouble."

The remark hit a nerve and stung. "City girl? You say that as if it were an insult." Maggie glared at him.

Drake shrugged his shoulders. "I say it because you've proven to me, once again, that city girls like you don't have the common sense to survive out here. No one who has any sense about them would come up an unfamiliar mountain trail alone and unarmed. To top it all off, it was nearly dusk when you set out. Did you even bring a flashlight?"

Maggie felt ashamed to admit, even to herself, she had planned her trip so poorly. "No, I didn't."

"Well, there you go," he said as if her answer proved his point.

"I thought you would understand," disappointment edged her words.

"Understand?" Drake gave a small huff. "What I understand is that you let your emotions cloud your judgment."

Maggie's hands flew to her hips. "There's nothing wrong with my judgment."

Drake crossed his arms over his chest and leaned back on his heels. "No? Tell me then. According to your judgment, what are the dangers you could face out here alone and unarmed?"

Maggie took a passing glance out to the dark forest of trees beyond the light of the fire. "Bears and snakes, mostly."

"Is that all?" He took another step closer.

"And mountain cats."

"And?"

"What do you want me to say Drake?"

"You're forgetting one of the most dangerous creatures of all."

"What would that be?" She nervously rubbed her

palms together and swallowed hard as he closed the distance between them.

"Man."

Maggie began to shake when her imagination started to roll.

"That possibility ever cross your mind?" He raised his hand to brush his knuckles across her cheek. "A beautiful young woman like you? All alone," he said deeply as his eyes lowered to her lips.

Maggie backed out of his reach. She retreated all the way to the cinderblock wall of the storage building, yet he kept coming. He braced his arms on either side of her, pressing her tight to the cold, unyielding wall. Something awakened deep inside her. A new awareness stole her breath and an emerging longing lodged in her throat until he bent his head and whispered close to her ear, "I come across men out here all the time that would love to have you in this position."

The cold reality of his words slammed into her. His words pierced through her stubborn pride. He was right. She had been a fool to come up here alone and unarmed.

"Not so sure of yourself now are you?" He asked as he continued to use his weight to hold her captive against the wall.

Maggie dropped her head in defeat but Drake wouldn't let her eyes stay down. He lifted her chin with his thumb. "Look at me." His command left no room for question. She reluctantly looked into his accusing eyes.

"Tell me you were wrong to come here alone." Drake held himself rigid as he made his demand.

"I..." Maggie lost her voice as warring emotions gagged her. She understood his point but couldn't bring herself to admit it.

She watched as a muscle twitched in his jaw, the only indication of his underlying anger as he held her with steely control. Common sense would have told her to be afraid of him. But, she instinctively knew Drake wouldn't hurt her. She even felt protected by his closeness, shielded from the dangers that lay beyond the firelight.

Maggie lifted her trembling hands to his waist, not to push him away, but to draw from his unyielding strength. He stiffened at her touch and pulled away a fraction of an inch.

"You're looking to the wrong place if you want to be comforted," Drake ground out the words and suddenly stepped away. Cold air filled the gap between them, leaving Maggie shivering in the void.

Drake continued to drill her. "Would it have helped Stephen if you had gotten yourself lost out here tonight?"

"No." Maggie averted her eyes. She looked into the dwindling fire without really seeing it.

"Would it have helped him if you had gotten bitten by a snake you couldn't see because you didn't have a flashlight?"

Maggie began to feel dizzy as his words chipped away at her defenses. She nearly choked on the words, "No. I didn't think about those things. I was focused on helping Stephen." She raised her moistened eyes to his. "He was so scared, Drake. I saw the fear in his eyes and I knew," Maggie paused, "I knew I couldn't live with myself if I didn't do everything I possibly could to help him."

"You were wrong to come up here alone, Maggie."

The wind shifted slightly, sending the thick campfire smoke spiraling in her direction. It singed her throat and burned her eyes. She waved her hands to clear the air and took a step to the side. She coughed through the words, "Then tell me what I should've done."

"You should have followed my rules."

"And not trust my own judgment at all?" She grasped for something within herself she could rely on.

Maggie sensed her defensive words had only fueled his anger. A dangerous fury filled his eyes as he slowly shook his head. "You should've learned not to trust your own judgment the moment you caught your betrothed in bed with another woman."

Maggie recoiled and sucked in a deep breath. Shockwaves filled with pain and humiliation slammed into her. His words cut her to the core and brought back the horror of finding Nathan in bed with the woman whose name she still didn't know. The raw intensity of the pain felt as sharp as when she had first discovered the truth. The small amount of confidence she had earned back in the past few days shattered, leaving a gaping hole of insecurity and fear deep inside. She couldn't breathe. She couldn't speak. Tears sprang to her eyes as Drake continued to glare at her.

Did the man not have a heart? Maggie took a few more steps to the side and drew in another deep breath of the cool, crisp air trying to push down the painful emotions swirling to the surface. She held her arms tight across her middle to ward off the pain.

Drake held a solemn expression as his eyes trailed over her. A trace of concern creased his brow, but he spoke no apologies. Maggie abruptly turned away to take refuge in the storage building.

"Maggie."

She heard Drake call her in a hushed tone but chose to ignore it. She chose to ignore him. She thought she had done the right thing by coming up here, just like she thought she had been doing the right thing with Nathan. But once again, she had been proven wrong.

****

Drake unclenched his jaw and his features softened as his initial anger dissolved into traces of guilt. He wanted her to understand how reckless she had been. He wanted to keep her from making the same errors in judgment again. He had expected to feel satisfaction when he broke her defenses. Yet, he only felt ashamed at the route he had taken. He had ripped open her thin layer of protection, exposing her recent wounds in order to drive home his point.

He kicked a rock, sending it scattering across the clearing. No matter how angry he had been, or ever could be at her, he had no right to use her own hurts against her. He could only imagine the fresh wave of pain he had just put her through.

Drake stared into the fire as he clenched his fists. Some protector he turned out to be. She had been better off before he had arrived. She made it here on her own, against the odds and without any help. An ironic smile tugged at his lips. She turned out to be stronger and more courageous than he ever expected her to be.

A cool breeze stirred the air, hitting the beads of perspiration that dotted his forehead. A chill ran down his body and jiggled his thoughts away. He needed to get out of his sweat drenched clothes before the cold seeped down to his core. He looked at the dim light glowing from within the storage building. He had to face Maggie, and he had to do it now.

Drake pulled off his damp shirt as he walked inside. He looked down the long, narrow hallway but didn't see Maggie. That meant only one thing. She had to be in the sleeping area. His mouth went dry at the thought of approaching her.

He quickly changed into a set of clean clothes that he had on one of the shelves near the door, while listening for any sounds from Maggie. Silence came from within the building, while a rumble of thunder came from outside. The wind knocked a low lying branch against the window. It chafed against the glass, warning Drake of an approaching storm.

Drake could sense it, he could smell it. The wind

kicked up a notch and the forest critters became quiet, no doubt searching for cover. The smell of rain freshened air came in through the open doorway. He went back outside to gather his backpack, and noticed the opened bag of marshmallows on the ground. He scooped up the bag and closed it with his fist.

As he had climbed up the mountain, fear for Maggie's safety had consumed his thoughts and a rush of adrenaline had kept him climbing the trail with reckless abandon. He had stumbled on images of her hurt or lost all the way up until he found her sitting quietly roasting marshmallows. Over a fire that she had built herself.

"What did you expect?" he mumbled to himself. *To find her frightened and alone. To find her needing my help.* His answer bothered him more than he cared to admit when he realized he wanted her to need him.

He ground his teeth as he sucked in the wind-blown air. He lifted his head and looked to the building housing Maggie. With his own motives in question, he closed his eyes and sought guidance from the Lord. *Please let me know what to say to her. Show me how to guide her to You. Use me to bring her closer to You, and closer to the healing she needs.*

As the approaching storm blew leaves around in circles at his feet, he felt God's presence surround him. A sense of peace came over him, and the last traces of his anger vanished.

Lightning flashed and the rain dropped in heavy, solid drops to the ground. Drake dashed for cover. He closed the door behind him, blocking out the driving wind and rain, and opening him to the quiet stillness once again. The cool, dank air inside contrasted with the fresh, rain-bitten air outside. He took a moment to adjust and looked down the narrow passageway. He prayed once again he would say the right things to her.

Drake ran his fingers through his hair and took the first step toward her. His pace quickened with each step he took, his stride lengthening. Anticipation grew as he stepped around the corner to face her.

"Maggie." He found her curled up on the cot asleep. A rush of air left his lungs, both in disappointment and in relief.

He squatted down next to her and gently swept a few strands of hair from her face. Her cheeks were still wet with fallen tears, and he brushed his thumbs across them. Guilt, strong and swift, coursed through his veins.

With her guard down, Maggie looked vulnerable and soft. Protective instincts rose in him again as he slipped a cover up over her shoulders. He walked away in silence, with a storm brewing in his heart as the lightning flashed and thunder cracked outside.

Chapter Eleven

Maggie woke with a sense of dread. Confusion took hold of her for a moment before she remembered what had happened. She buried her face in her hands and let out a long, slow breath. Drake had been angry with her last night, and now she had to face him again this morning.

She ran a hand through her tussled hair and dug inside her backpack for her hairbrush. As she brushed out her tangles she swallowed, trying to moisten her dry throat. Her eyes felt a little swollen and raw so she went to the sink to throw water on her face, and she drank a sip to ease the dryness in her throat.

She wondered how Drake would react to her this morning as she headed down the narrow passageway. She hoped his burning anger had cooled during the night. She stopped at the door and said a silent prayer, *Lord, please help me to face Drake and guide me as to what to say to him.* When she mustered up enough nerve, she stepped outside and immediately smelled freshly cooked bacon and saw Drake in front of the fire-pit. He had a fire going and had a pan of eggs frying over the flames. If she hadn't been so emotionally sore from the night before, she would have been impressed.

She stepped into the woods for some privacy, carrying her much appreciated toilet paper with her. When she returned, she couldn't bring herself to meet his eyes. She sat at the table with her back to him and shuffled through her backpack. She pulled out hand cleanser and washed her hands, then continued looking in her backpack for nothing in particular. She wanted to appear busy and distracted hoping it would make it easier to avoid him. She should've known better.

Drake walked over and sat directly across from her, making it impossible to ignore him. He set the pan of eggs on the table, added a plate of bacon next to it and said, "I know you're hungry, and I know you're hurting. I intend to fix both."

Maggie's eyes shot up to his. Concern etched his face and his anger from the night before seemed to have disappeared. She glanced down at the eggs and bacon and asked, "I see how you can fix the first, but the second?"

"I won't condone what you did Maggie, and I won't change my mind about it. But, I am sorry I hurt you."

Maggie sucked in a deep breath, dropped her backpack on the ground and nearly fainted. She couldn't believe Drake Strong had just apologized to her. She looked into his sincere eyes and felt her heart race with hope. She didn't think she had it in her to fight with him today, now maybe she didn't have to.

She admitted, "I'm surprised to hear you say that."

"I shouldn't have said what I did about your fiancé. I know how much it hurts."

She saw a glimpse of compassion in his expression. "You do?"

He nodded his head and scooted the plate with the bacon on it in front of them. "I only have this one plate to use. I hope you don't mind sharing."

She managed to shake her head. "It's fine. It smells good."

Drake scooped the fried eggs out of the pan and placed them on the plate with the bacon. He handed her a fork. Maggie took a bite of egg and savored it.

She asked, "Why does food taste better when you eat it outside?"

"I don't know, but it seems to doesn't it?" He grinned at her.

She reached up to grab a slice of bacon and brushed her knuckles against his. A sudden sense of intimacy warmed her, and she pulled her hand away. She glanced up at him to see if he had noticed, but he seemed to be intent on his food. As they ate, Maggie thought about apologizing to Drake. He had taken the first step and apologized to her and even made breakfast for her. She chewed on her bacon as she contemplated it.

Drake asked, "How are you feeling today?"

Her eyebrows lifted. She swallowed her food and said, "I'm okay, but a little sore from running up a mountain."

"I thought you might be sore. Do you think you're up for a little extra walk to the waterfall? It's worth seeing."

Maggie nearly dropped her fork at his kind offer. "Sounds good."

After they finished eating, she cleaned the dishes as Drake put out the fire. She rummaged in her pack for her toothbrush as he tidied up the camp. A few minutes later they headed for the waterfall remaining silent as they walked.

After a short hike, Maggie heard the rumble of the waterfall.

"It's right around the corner," Drake said.

When Maggie saw the waterfall she smiled. "It's gorgeous!" She watched a powerful stream of water cascading over an outcropping of rocks. The foliage on either side outlined the crystal clear falls. Rocks and boulders lay strewn at the bottom and a healthy stream took the water further down the mountain.

"I can't even imagine owning such a beautiful place," Maggie commented.

"Do you like it here?"

"I love it."

Drake seemed to be pleased by her answer, and

he walked to a dry boulder across from the waterfall and took a seat. He indicated for her to sit next to him so she did. He picked up a long stick and drew circles in the dirt with the tip of it.

"I had a fiancé once," he admitted as he studied the stick in front of him.

"What happened?"

He shrugged his shoulders and remained silent for a while as he watched the waterfall.

Maggie said, "I understand if you don't want to talk about it. When I broke off the engagement with Nathan, I had to call my family and friends and tell them not to come for the wedding. It was one of the hardest things I've had to do. They asked me so many questions. Questions I didn't want to have to answer."

"It was a little different for me," Drake said. "We hadn't even set a date yet."

Maggie lifted her knees and hugged them. She willed Drake to say more but didn't ask. If he had a fiancé once, maybe he really did understand the pain she had been going through.

Drake dropped the stick and said, "I don't put the blame on either one of us for the break-up. Circumstances drew us apart."

"Did you meet her here?"

"No." Drake shook his head and smirked. "She wouldn't set foot out here. She's a city girl through and through. I was living in the city when I met her, but I always wanted to move to the country. I'm not much for crowds."

"There's a shocker." Maggie laughed. She felt encouraged when he returned her smile.

"Not surprised, huh?"

"Nope. Why did you break up?"

"I inherited this land from my father."

"Your father? I thought Aunt Cammie raised you?"

"She did. I never knew him. He left my mother

when she found out she was pregnant with me." Drake's jaw tensed. "As far as I know, he never even came to see me after I was born. I don't know why he left the land to me. I suppose he didn't have anyone else to give it to. I'll probably never know. But, when I found out about it, I prayed about what to do. It took several months for me to decide. I felt that God was calling me here. I knew I wanted out of the city. I asked Kara to come with me. She wouldn't even consider it."

"Did she know how you felt? That God wanted you here?"

"Yes. But she still refused to come."

"What did you do?"

"I came here and spent a year trying to build a place she might be content with. I hoped she would change her mind and come with me. When I was finished with the resort, I went to see her." Drake ran a hand through his hair. "She had already married someone else."

"Oh Drake, I'm so sorry." Maggie's heart ached for him. "You held on to your hope for a year. You must have really loved her."

"I thought so at the time. Now I realize that it was never meant to be."

"So you decorated the cabins so nicely for her?"

He nodded his head.

Maggie wondered what it would be like to have a man love her enough to do something like that for her. "She missed out by not coming here with you," she said softly.

Drake's eyes snapped to hers and surprise marked his features. He studied her for a moment before looking back at the waterfall.

"Do you ever think about what would have happened if you had stayed in the city?" Maggie asked when he didn't say anything else.

"Yes. Every day of that first year I asked myself if I had made the right decision."

"And?"

"Deep down, I already knew the answer. I knew God had been calling me to a different life for some time. I knew it before I proposed to her. If I made a mistake it was asking her to marry me in the first place." Drake leaned back on his hands before he explained, "I worked in security after I got out of the military. My career was in the city and I didn't see any way out at the time." Drake looked at Maggie. "I didn't trust God to open the doors for me so I could do what he was calling me to do."

"But then you inherited the land and decided to move?"

"Yes. When the doors finally opened, I went for it. But Kara didn't fit into my new life."

"Are you glad you made that decision?"

"To follow God's leading? Yes. Absolutely. I would've eventually resented Kara for keeping me where I didn't belong, and she would have resented me if she came out here. It's better this way."

Maggie stretched out her legs and said, "You sound so logical and matter of fact. I can't see things as clearly as you do."

"I didn't come to this conclusion overnight. Give yourself some time."

She looked at the man who she would have sworn just last night didn't have a heart inside his body. Now she knew he did have a heart and it had been broken once, maybe under different circumstances, but broken just the same. Maggie decided that he may not be a barbarian after all.

"I'm sorry Drake."

"Don't be. It was a long time ago."

"No. I mean…I'm sorry I didn't listen to you. I'm sorry I came up here alone. You were only trying to protect me. I should've listened to you."

Their eyes locked in mutual understanding. Drake gave her a small smile but the serious tone in his voice remained as he said, "I'm glad you understand that I'm trying to keep you safe." He reached up to her face and smoothed a few strands of hair from her eyes. "I don't want you to get hurt."

A spark of attraction jolted through Maggie at his touch. His fingers left traces of fire on her skin and his softly spoken words opened hidden emotions within her. He had revealed a personal piece of his life to her, a piece that made her understand that he, too, had deeper emotions within him. Drake had suffered losses and heartache and had to make difficult decisions in his life, just as she had. She suddenly saw him as more than a stubborn, overbearing man. She saw a glimpse of the kinder, gentler man that lay beneath his tough exterior.

She let her guard down, no longer afraid of the harsh man she had thought him to be. Her breath caught in her throat as she looked at him for the first time without having her defenses up. Her attraction to him filtered beyond that of his rugged appearance and handsome features. It went deeper down to the true man that lay beneath. Her heart lurched, and she knew she had lost a part of her own heart to him. For a moment, she let herself imagine how his lips would feel on hers, and her eyes wandered down to where her mind had taken her.

Drake suddenly looked away from her as if he could read her mind and stood abruptly. His tone turned businesslike. "We should head back down to the cabins. I want to get an update on Stephen. Do you want to walk the long way down or take the zip line?"

Maggie answered without hesitation, "The zip line."

She leapt off the rock and started walking away from him. What had she been thinking? She had practically drooled on Drake Strong's well-worn boots just because he had opened up to her a little and shown her a touch of compassion. She wondered what he must think of her. After all, just because he didn't want to see her hurt, didn't mean he welcomed her here anymore today than he did when she had first arrived.

****

A few hours after they had arrived back at the resort, Drake stood in front of the bulletin board rearranging the schedule. He had called the hospital to check on Stephen and found out he was doing fine and planned to return to the resort within a few days. He had also checked the weather forecast. They called for a rainstorm to move in tomorrow so he had to change the cave trip to the following week. He had a hard time trying to concentrate as he adjusted the schedule as his thoughts drifted to Maggie. He still didn't know why he had told her about Kara. He never discussed his personal life with his guests. At least not until Maggie came along.

He caught himself smiling at her bravery in going up the mountain alone. With her being unaccustomed to the mountains, he knew it took a lot of courage to do it. It still amazed him that she would do something so courageous and yet so foolish. It had been the foolish part that had driven him to such anger. He realized that behind the anger had been fear. Fear for her safety. He didn't know when he had started to care for her, but his reaction yesterday had proven it beyond a doubt. Then today at the waterfall, it had taken all of his willpower to keep from kissing her when she looked at him without her shield of protection up. She had a contagious warmth in her eyes that had spread through him, softening his well guarded heart.

He stood for a moment, staring at the bulletin board but not really seeing it. He said a quick prayer, *Lord, please help me to know where Maggie fits into my life, if at all.*

Aunt Cammie ambled into the kitchen and made a ruckus pulling out a large pot from under the counter. She said, "I hope you weren't too hard on her."

Drake finished working on the board and walked into the kitchen. "I was," he admitted.

Aunt Cammie turned disapproving eyes toward him as she set the pot on the stove. "You need to know something Drake, and I want you to listen good." She placed her hands on her hips in a way that Drake recognized from his adolescent years. He knew she meant business so he focused on her and listened intently.

"That girl came running when she heard the screaming. She got here before I even got out the door. Oh, Beverly was making an awful racket, hollering and such. The poor dear had been so afraid for her husband. Anyway," Aunt Cammie shifted her weight from one foot to the other and continued, "Maggie stepped up right away and took charge. When I came out the door, she was telling Stephen to stay still, just like you told her. Throughout the ruckus, she stayed calm and level-headed. She kept to what you said, Drake. After she told him to stay still, she demanded someone find you. Just like you said to do. I even tried to put a cold bag of peas on his leg and she stopped me. She said you told them not to do it, she didn't even know why, but since you said it, she insisted we not do it. Every step of the way, she kept to your rules."

"Except when she went up the mountain alone," Drake pointed out.

"She said she knew you wouldn't want her to go alone so that's when she asked Dillon to go with her. She tried to follow your rules, but apparently Dillon backed out on her."

Drake thought about what Aunt Cammie said. Guilt flowed into him again at his harsh reaction, but he knew he had to stand firm. "She should have come back with him."

Aunt Cammie agreed, "Yes, she should've. But

can you see how such a compassionate woman couldn't turn back. She did what she needed to do."

"I understand that. But she put herself in danger."

She looked at him and narrowed her eyes. Then a smile played at her lips. "I see now. I knew you would like her. I knew it the first time I saw her."

Drake cleared his throat. "She's a guest. She's only going to be around here for a few days. I know you want me to find someone, but don't get your hopes up. She's a city dweller, just like…" he trailed off, not wanting to bring up his ex-fiancé's name.

"Oh no you don't mister. She's nothing like Kara and don't you forget it. You need to smooth things over with Maggie." She softened her voice and added, "Give her a chance Drake."

He nodded and headed for the door. "I'll think about it." He stepped outside knowing his aunt wanted him to be happy, but he also knew from experience that city dwellers didn't fit into his world no matter how much he wanted them to.

Drake spotted Maggie near the woodpile, swinging the axe at a piece of wood and his pulse kicked up its speed. He looked at her smooth, practiced movements and couldn't see any part of the citified woman he thought she was. For a moment, it looked like she belonged out here in his wilderness. With him.

He quickly pushed down his wishful thoughts and walked over near her, careful to avoid the swinging axe. He crossed his arms over his chest and leaned against the storage shed, watching her in silence until she looked up at him.

"Hi," she said with a breathtaking smile. She took laboring breaths that made her chest rise and fall in exertion.

He felt his world turn on its side as he looked at her. It took all of his effort to keep his eyes on her face and not let them roam down the length of her.

He had a sudden urge to pull her into his arms and kiss her senseless. Instead, he cleared his throat and said, "Aunt Cammie told me how you followed what I told you to do in case of a snake bite."

She nodded. "Yeah. I remembered what you told us to do. I know you didn't think I was listening, but I was," she said as she set the axe down next to a log.

"I know you listened to me Maggie, and I want you to know I appreciate it." He saw surprise register on her face. He also saw a glimpse of something else. For the first time, he detected a need for acceptance in her eyes.

He pushed away from the storage shed and stepped near her. He turned to face her and said, "I know what you think. But you're wrong." He took her hand in his and gave it a gentle squeeze. He liked the way her warm, slender hand felt tucked inside his grasp, and he let it linger there for a moment.

He lowered his voice, leaned in close to her and admitted, "I do like you Maggie."

Astonishment swept across her features and her mouth nearly dropped open before he let go of her hand and picked up the axe to continue chopping firewood where she had left off.

Maggie moved aside to sit on a larger log and watched him as he split the logs with ease.

She had just started to say something to him when the sound of a rumbling engine caught their attention. They both looked up at the same time as Harley's seaplane flew across the sky.

"Harley's not due back yet. I wonder what he's doing here," Drake spoke his thoughts aloud.

After Harley settled his craft at the dock and climbed out, he moseyed toward Aunt Cammie's Kitchen and waved at Maggie and Drake before disappearing inside.

Drake returned his attention to the dock as a

tall, well-dressed man climbed from the seaplane. The man stepped out with an air of entitlement as he scanned the resort. Arrogance showed through his smile as his eyes landed on Maggie.

"Mags!" The man shouted and waved.

Drake turned to look at Maggie and saw recognition in her features. He watched as all traces of color drained from her flushed face and fear sparked in her eyes. She took a reflexive step backward. Drake's defenses came to full alert. He needed no introduction to know Maggie's ex-fiancé had just found her.

Drake stepped close to her and placed a reassuring hand at the small of her back. He watched as Maggie turned and looked to him for guidance. The insecurity he saw in her eyes caused a strong surge of protectiveness to course through him.

She had more than earned his respect with her charitable actions and show of compassion in the few days that he had known her. She had put an impression on him that would be difficult, if not impossible, to cast aside. Nathan had no right to put fear into her eyes. No man did. Anger fueled his blood and his jaw clenched as he pulled Maggie closer.

Drake became motionless; stunned at the turn his own thoughts had taken. When had he begun to think of her as something other than his temporary guest? He couldn't pin-point the time, but he knew it had happened.

Maggie tore her imploring gaze from his before lifting her chin, squaring her shoulders and setting off toward the dock.

"Maggie," Drake's voice commanded her reply.

She turned briefly as she kept walking and said, "It's okay, Drake. I need this to be finished once and for all."

If it weren't for the truth in Maggie's words,

Drake wouldn't let her ex-fiancé anywhere near her. He felt an unfamiliar surge of possessiveness as he watched her stride up to the man who had almost become her husband. Jealousy blindsided him at the familiar way the man's eyes perused her. Drake's muscles constricted as he dropped the axe and moved closer to the dock. He waited far enough away to give Maggie the space she needed, but close enough to protect her.

Chapter Twelve

Maggie approached Nathan as he stood at the end of the dock and asked abruptly, "What are you doing here?" Her business-like tone remained as detached as her emotions.

"Mags." He smiled. "What else? I came to bring you home." He stepped to her and hugged her without invitation.

"You wasted your time. I'm not going anywhere with you." Maggie stood rigid, refusing to return his hug. When he pulled away, she studied him and recognized that any appeal he once held for her had been destroyed with his betrayal.

She cast a glance over her shoulder. Drake had moved close to the dock and stood with his arms crossed over his chest and feet wide apart. He glared at Nathan, not bothering to hide the contempt in his eyes. Reassured, Maggie turned back to face Nathan as he began to speak.

"Babe, listen. I came all the way here to see you. To work things out. I cleared my schedule and took the time to come and get you."

"So I should be honored that you put aside your busy life to interrupt mine?"

"My time is valuable, Magdalene." His brow creased as he spoke.

Maggie bristled. "It's all about you isn't it Nathan? It always has been."

"I had hoped in the few days since you left you would've come to see things differently." He blew out a deep, impatient breath.

Maggie's mouth dropped open. "Come to see things differently? Did you actually come here expecting me to leave with you? To still marry you?" Her hands turned into fists and found their way to her hips.

His smile disappeared and his voice took on a gruff tone as he asked, "Why shouldn't I? You've done everything else I've ever asked you to do. Well, almost everything." He made a cursory glance down her body.

Disgust ran through Maggie and she turned to leave. Nathan grabbed her arm, halting her retreat.

Drake's deep voice vibrated across the space that separated them, "Hands off."

She noticed Nathan's temple throbbing at an irregular pace as he looked at Drake. "This is none of your concern."

"Maggie's my guest. That makes it my concern," Drake stated as he took a few steps out onto the dock. "Let go."

Nathan studied Drake for a moment before returning his eyes to Maggie. He reluctantly dropped her arm.

"So, you two got something going on?"

"My life is none of your business now."

"That's where you're wrong. I have too much invested in you to let you go."

"So I'm an investment now?" Maggie tilted her head.

"I'm a business man Maggie. You always knew that," Nathan ground out the words. "I have a need and I fill it with whatever or whomever I choose."

"What kind of need do you think you have for me?"

"I need a beautiful woman in my arms that my colleagues would envy me for without the hassle of someone who wants something back from me. You're not like most women I know. You never asked for anything back Maggie. You're the perfect solution to my problem."

"What we had was only business to you? I

thought what we had was personal. Do you even know what that means?"

"I know what it means to be personal with a woman. You saw that firsthand Maggie."

She felt like the boards under her feet began to slip away. She widened her stance to remain steady under his hurtful words. "Why did you sleep with her?"

His eyes narrowed and he scoffed as he looked her over. "Did you actually think I would be content with only you for the rest of my life?"

Nathan's words slammed into Maggie taking her breath away and battering her confidence even further. She looked at Drake and took a step closer to him as pain seared her heart. Drake's eyes looked wild and dangerous as he kept them focused on Nathan.

Nathan glared at Drake before returning his eyes to her. "You want him. I see it in your eyes. What could he possibly offer you that I can't?"

She lifted her chin and replied, "He's more of a man than you could ever hope to be."

Nathan's nostrils flared as his face heated. Anger seeped through his words as he said, "You ungrateful..." He lifted his hand as if to strike her.

The next few seconds turned into a blur. Drake moved on Nathan with swift, unrelenting force. He had Nathan on his knees with his arm twisted behind his back before Maggie knew what had happened.

The dock rocked under the tussle and Maggie lost her balance. She stepped back to regain control but found herself too close to the edge. She tumbled back, falling into the cold lake water. Shock coursed through her as the water enveloped her, soaking her clothes, shoes and coat. The weight of the material pulled her down and she struggled for the surface that lay beyond her reach. She futilely kicked with her sodden shoes, as panic grabbed her chest and squeezed tight.

An explosion of bubbles erupted near her as someone dove in beside her. A strong arm wrapped around her shoulders from behind and a hard body pressed against her back. She saw the rippling surface come closer and closer as the man hauled her upward. When she finally broke the surface, she gulped in air while heaving coughs erupted from her lungs.

"It's okay. I've got you," Drake said close to her ear. "Relax and let me take you to shore."

Maggie let herself be pulled over to the shallow water and tried her best not to struggle in Drake's arms. He moved swiftly as he helped her completely out of the water and removed her drenched coat. They collapsed onto the grass and Maggie turned into Drake's embrace. He held her tight against him and issued reassuring words to her.

She felt Drake stiffen as she heard footsteps approaching. In her sudden panic, she had forgotten about Nathan. Drake lifted her up with him as he came to his feet, supporting her with an arm around her waist. She saw Nathan approaching in his untouched, dry clothes. She realized that while Drake had risked his life to save her, Nathan hadn't even gotten a toe wet.

"Are you okay?" Nathan asked warily, staying a few feet away from them.

She eyed him skeptically and hugged tighter to Drake. "I will be when you accept that what you want from me isn't going to happen."

"I never intended to hurt you," he said with a touch of remorse.

"Maybe not. But you did intend to use me," Maggie's body shook as she said the words. Whether it was only from being dressed in freezing wet clothes, or if her sudden anger added to the shaking, she didn't know. But, as she spoke the shaking became stronger, more violent. "You tried to force me into being someone I'm not."

"You seemed willing enough to me."

Drake began rubbing her arms to warm her. She kept her focus on Nathan. "We would have been miserable together. Can't you see that? You can't force yourself to love someone, Nathan. You don't love me. Why would you want to be married to someone you don't love? To someone who doesn't love you?"

"Marriage doesn't need love to be successful."

Maggie shook her head. "I almost feel sorry for you. I don't know if God has someone planned for you. But I do know that if He does, that someone isn't me."

The kitchen door opened and Aunt Cammie stepped out bellowing, "What in tarnation is going on out here?"

Harley followed her outside carrying a piece of pie on a plate. He watched the commotion with curiosity, but stayed quiet as he continued to eat.

Drake called out, "It's okay Aunt Cammie. Harley's just about to take Nathan home. His business here is finished."

Maggie watched Aunt Cammie scramble back into the kitchen. Harley nodded at Drake and shoveled down the rest of his pie before heading back to the plane.

Nathan looked weary and confused as he said, "I could have given you a good life."

"You don't get it, do you? I do have a good life."

Aunt Cammie came outside toting two blankets. She hastily made her way over to them. "Maggie, you'd best be getting dry. The air is chilly and I don't want you to take sick on us now. You're lips are already turning blue," she warned.

"Thanks." She accepted the offered blanket and pulled it up over her shoulders. She watched Drake as he did the same.

"It's over Nathan," Drake growled, looking as

dangerous as any wild animal in the forest. "I'll walk you back to the plane. Maggie, go get some dry clothes on. I'll come by later to check on you," he said with authority.

She looked into Nathan's eyes one last time and said, "Goodbye Nathan."

Sadness covered her heart, weighing her down as heavy as the wet clothes she still wore. She had once thought he was the one for her. Discovering how wrong she had been not only saddened her, but sent a spiral of panic up into her chest. How could she ever trust her judgment again?

Maggie watched as Aunt Cammie went back inside her kitchen and Drake walked Nathan down the dock. Drake strode with a clear purpose in mind, while Nathan showed reluctance in leaving. When they reached the floating platform, Drake stepped close to Nathan and said something so low she could only guess at the words. Nathan's pallor turned sheer white, and he backed away from Drake. He gave Maggie a fleeting glance before disappearing inside the plane.

Chapter Thirteen

Maggie changed into dry clothes and lit the fire in the fireplace. Her cabin came to life with the crackling flame and the resulting glow warmed the room along with the actual heat from the fire. She soon felt her solid shaking give way to smaller, less frequent shivers. Her chattering teeth quieted as she settled on the couch and pulled a warm throw across her shoulders.

She replayed what had happened with Nathan in her mind. As she thought about the events, what Drake had done for her overshadowed all other memories. She pictured him standing on the end of the dock, poised and ready to protect her. She remembered the fury in his eyes when Nathan had hurt her with his words and how fast he had blocked Nathan's hand when he had moved to strike her. Drake had even jumped into the water to rescue her, without reservations or hesitation.

The need to belong pulled at her heart and hope began to grow. He had admitted he liked her. Maybe he had also begun to accept her being here.

A brisk knock on her door interrupted the quiet in the cabin.

"Are you ready for me?"

Drake's question took Maggie by surprise. Was she ready for him? He would have more questions for her. Questions she may not have the answers to. She took a deep breath and answered, "Yes, come in."

Drake let himself in, carrying two mugs of steaming hot liquid. She noticed he had changed into clean, dry clothes.

"I brought some hot chocolate," he said as he walked over to the couch and sat down close to her. He had shaved and showered, the scent of soap still clung to his skin. His leg brushed against hers and a welcoming shiver steadily climbed up her side.

"Are you still cold?"

Maggie shook her head as she sipped the hot chocolate. "No."

"I felt you shivering."

Maggie's face flushed as she brought her eyes to his. "Yes, I did shiver. But it's not because I'm cold."

She felt a new heat radiate from his body and saw the intensity of his gaze deepen with her answer. She looked away, not knowing what to make of her attraction to Drake or her boldness in letting him know with her words. She took a sip of the hot chocolate and redirected her thoughts.

"Thanks for jumping into the lake after me."

His eyes locked with hers as he said, "Not coming after you was never an option."

A new set of tingles made their way into her heart and she turned her eyes from him, afraid he may see right through her. She looked into the fire and continued, "When I fell into the water, I panicked. I had never felt anything so paralyzing before. I know how to swim, I just..." her voice trailed off when she looked at him again and saw his eyes had softened with compassion.

"The shock of the cold water is enough to knock the senses out of you. Even the best swimmers can drown when caught off guard like that."

"Nathan was going to hit me."

"Yes, he was."

Maggie saw tension ripple through Drake's features as he finished his drink in two long swallows. He erupted from the couch, walked over to the fire and knelt next to the hearth. He picked up a log and jammed it into the flames causing sparks to fly and ashes to sift through the grate.

Maggie felt the shift in Drake's mood and rose from the couch to sit next to him. She watched the hungry flames devour the new piece of wood before bringing her eyes up to his. Confused emotions spiraled through her. "When I first met him, I never thought he would raise his hand to me. He seemed like such a gentleman."

Drake dusted off his hands and sat on the hearth as his hardened expression softened.

She sighed, "Nathan threw my life into chaos. He used me. I don't even feel like the same person on the inside anymore. Everything I thought I knew, everything I thought I could rely on turned out to be false. A hoax. I put my hopes and dreams into what turned out to be an illusion."

"You put your hopes and dreams into a human being, Maggie. Humans have faults, none of us are void of sin."

"You're defending him," she accused.

Drake's eyes narrowed and his voice lowered. "Not at all. There's no excuse for what he did. What I'm trying to say is that God needs to be your foundation. The One you lean on. Then, when people let you down, you're not left without a solid core."

She ran her hands over her face and looked back at Drake. "I guess I learned that the hard way."

He nodded his head. "Learning the hard way has the most impact on our lives doesn't it?"

"Yes, it does." She shivered. "I'm sorry Nathan came here and caused trouble for you. I didn't really expect him to find me here. I knew he could if he wanted to. But I didn't really expect it."

"I'm glad he found you."

"What? Why?" Maggie gasped.

"Because now he knows he has no choice but to let you go. Now, you can go back to civilization and not worry about him coming after you. You're free to start a new life without having to look over your shoulder for him."

Maggie soaked in his words. "You're right." Relief spread through her and a smile erupted on her lips. "I am free." Then the smile faded as fast as it had come. "But I still don't know what I should do. Where do I go? I don't want to go back to L.A. And going home to Texas would be like giving up on my dream."

Drake drew his legs in, leaned forward and steepled his fingers together. He waited in silence for her to continue.

Maggie fought the tears that threatened her and said, "I had a thriving business, a nice apartment and an overall satisfying life. Nathan took it all away from me, and I didn't even see it coming. I feel so foolish."

"Sometimes it's hard to see that you're taking the wrong path until it's too late. Sometimes, you're completely lost before you even realize you're going the wrong way."

"I never thought of life as a path before."

"Every decision you make leads you somewhere."

"That's true. But, how do I keep from going the wrong way when there are so many choices to make in life?"

"Pray and ask God to guide you," he answered simply.

"You make it sound so simple. You sound so confident, so assured. How do you do it? How do you go through life with the confidence of knowing your doing the right thing, making the right choices?" she asked as she scooted over to lean back on the couch.

Drake followed her. "I'm not always confident," he answered as he settled in next to her. "But I do walk with God and trust him to lead me. It's not always easy, but I know He'll keep me going in the right direction."

Maggie read the honesty in Drake's eyes. Admiration filled her as she realized he truly meant what he said. "I sure do need a lot of guidance. I've made some really bad decisions recently."

He gave her arm a playful nudge. "Don't be so hard on yourself. Think of it as a learning experience. What have you learned so far?"

"That's easy. Not to trust my own judgment, as you clearly pointed out to me yesterday when I went up the mountain for the anti-venom."

"I've been too hard on you."

"No. You've been great. You've been the one person who doesn't shy away from telling me the truth."

"I'm glad you see it that way. Listen, while we're talking about the truth, I want to ask you something," Drake lowered his voice and edged closer to her.

Maggie stiffened and asked hoarsely, "What?"

"After I pulled you out of the water, you told Nathan he didn't want to marry someone who doesn't love him. Is it true that you're not in love with him?"

She looked down at her fingers and nodded. "Yes. I thought I was at one time. But, you showed me that I never really loved him."

"I showed you? How?"

Maggie shrugged her shoulders and studied her toes.

"Tell me," Drake said in a low voice. He lifted her chin with his thumb, turning her head and coaxing her to meet his eyes.

"By making me feel things for you that I never did for him...or anyone else. Ever." Maggie gave a nervous laugh then said, "I can only imagine what you think of me now. After all, what kind of woman breaks up with her fiancé and is attracted to another man only a few days later?"

"You want to know what kind of woman I think you are? I think you're one of the most courageous women I've ever met. You face difficult situations head-on without a thought of retreating. When someone needs something, you do everything you can to try to help them. You stood up to me, Maggie. You stood up to Nathan. You're a strong, intelligent woman. Don't let anyone tell you otherwise." Drake turned to face her. "And, while I'm spilling my guts here, I'll admit that I've been attracted to you since the first moment I laid eyes on you."

His words jolted Maggie into a new awareness. "You have?"

Drake cupped her face in his hand and whispered, "Yes. And now that I've told you what I think, I'm going to show you what I feel."

****

Drake bent his head and tasted her lips for the first time. Sweet and soft, her lips molded to his perfectly. The kiss felt even better than he had imagined. And he had imagined kissing her many more times than he even cared to admit. He deepened the kiss and wrapped his free arm around her shoulder, pulling her close. She melted into him and he held her tight to his chest, reveling in her returned embrace.

His breath mingled with hers as he backed away an inch, only to come back to her and kiss her again and again. Each time his lips met hers, he became bolder. He kissed her with a rising need that mirrored the one he saw in her expression. Maggie awakened dormant emotions within him and tugged at the heart he had closed off over two years ago.

When he finally pulled away Maggie murmured, "Thanks, Drake."

His lips curled up as he said, "That's a first."

"What is?"

"A woman thanking me for kissing her." He let his hand drop from her face to caress the length of her slender arm. He kept holding her close, reluctant to let her go.

Her cheeks exploded in color and she said, "I

meant for talking to me. You've helped me. You've made me understand things I never understood before and made me feel things I never felt before."

She leaned into him and initiated another long lasting kiss. He let out a low groan as she let her fingers travel over his jaw line and down the nape of his neck. Finally, her palm explored his chest, sending shockwaves of electricity down his torso.

She broke the kiss, leaned into his embrace and asked, "What if I told you I don't want to leave here when the two weeks are over?"

Drake stiffened at her words. His heart turned stone cold. "Don't tell me things you don't mean."

Memories of Kara bombarded him. His heart and his hopes had been crushed by a woman who belonged in the city. He felt like a fool for having a weakness for another woman who didn't fit into his world. Regret washed through him along with a wave of anger. Maggie had tugged on his heart and had begun to open it, when he had it reserved for a woman who belonged in his wilderness.

"But I do mean it," she said softly.

He wanted to believe her. But he knew better. "No. You can't. You're a city girl, remember?"

"But I like it here. And I like you. Why is that so hard for you to accept?"

"You've only been here a few days Maggie. How could you possibly know what it would be like to stay here?"

She leaned back and sent him a searching look as she let her hand continue to explore his chest. "I could find out. Drake, I want..."

He broke into her words and grabbed her wrist, instantly pulling her hand off of his chest. "I don't think you know what you want Maggie," Drake said with an edge to his voice. He saw the confusion spark in her eyes, but refused to let any guilt weaken his resolve.

"It seems to me you know what *you* want..."

Maggie began and brushed his lips with hers.

Drake pulled away. "Enough. I am a man Maggie." He let his eyes roam over her, exploring her curves and he swallowed. "Don't tempt me."

"I didn't mean..." Maggie withdrew from him suddenly. "I wouldn't..."

He saw her eyes widen and her mouth drop open as she realized what she had implied with her words. He stood and walked a few feet away, running a hand through his hair and said, "This isn't a good idea." He swore under his breath before adding, "I had no right to kiss you. I shouldn't even have let you come here in the first place."

"I thought you finally wanted me here. I thought..." Maggie looked to be on the verge of tears.

Drake confessed, "I am attracted to you, and I do like you. But, that doesn't change the fact that you wouldn't last out here, not for any length of time."

"What makes you say that?" Her eyes rounded and deepened. "It's because of Kara isn't it? You're pushing me away because of her," she paused then added, "I see the truth in your eyes, Drake."

"I learn from my mistakes, Maggie. I don't intend to make them a second time."

"I thought you had changed your mind about me. I thought you had finally accepted me coming here." Maggie wrapped the warm throw tighter around her.

Drake recognized her defensive gesture but refused to let her dissuade him. He shook his head and said, "You've mistaken my desire for acceptance." He stalked to the door and opened it. "I'm sorry if I mislead you." He closed the door to the cabin behind him, and then he closed the one guarding his heart.

Chapter Fourteen

The rain came the next day just has it had been forecasted. Maggie pulled the hood of her raincoat over her head as she stepped off of the porch. Dawn approached, promising to open up a brand new day, and Maggie needed to be ready for it. The only way she knew to get through her tangled emotions was to go to the kitchen and bake something sinful.

Her face heated as she remembered how Drake had turned away from her. Even after he had complemented her on her bravery and admitted he liked her and found her attractive, he still hadn't accepted her being there and probably never would.

A wave of embarrassment washed over her when she remembered how she had thrown herself at him with her loneliness spurring her forward. And what she had said to him, he must have thought she would jump into bed with him that very night. She didn't doubt she had lost his respect, because she had lost some of her own for herself.

"Maggie."

She almost didn't hear her name being spoken through her thoughts and the pelting rain. When she heard it a second time, she stopped and looked up. She stood in front of Drake's cabin. She looked up to his porch and into his penetrating eyes.

"We need to talk."

Maggie needed to get her hands into a pile of buttery flour before she could clear her mind enough to speak to him coherently. "Later." She tore her gaze from his expressive eyes and started walking up the path again.

Drake came down the steps two at a time and

took her arm. "No. Now," he commanded. Rain immediately soaked his clothes and ran in rivulets down his hair and face. He didn't seem to notice as he guided her with a firm grip up the steps and inside his cabin, not letting her have a chance to escape. He shut the door behind them before he let her go.

He swiped the raindrops from his eyes before he said, "About last night."

Maggie ducked her head and studied her wet boots. His finger dipped under her chin and lifted it until her eyes met his. Tears of embarrassment threatened her and she tried hard to keep her composure as she said, "I don't usually throw myself at men."

Drake smiled. "You've said that to me before."

Maggie remembered the incident when she threw herself at him after the zip line ride and a new wave of embarrassment assaulted her.

His temporary smile disappeared as he said, "I had no business kissing you. You're a guest at my resort, and I think it's best we keep things professional between us."

"It's a little late for that isn't it?"

Drake clenched his jaw and sighed. "Maggie…"

"Look, we both said and did things last night we regret. I want you to know I wouldn't have…" she paused, "What I mean is…I don't…"

"I understand."

"But…"

"I said I understand."

Maggie nodded. "Well then. You understand me and I certainly understand you."

"Do you?"

"I understand that you still don't accept my being here alone and that you don't want to like me, even if you do. I understand you don't want to be attracted to me, even if you are. So, you want to continue on as if nothing happened between us. Am I right?"

He shrugged. "Yeah."

Maggie reached back and opened the door behind her. Before she turned to leave she said, "Then consider it done." She stepped out the door and quietly closed it, hoping she could follow through with her promise.

****

Drake needed coffee, and he needed it now. Aggravated with himself for hurting her once again, he threw on his raincoat and jerked the hood on his head. He followed Maggie through the rain and into the kitchen.

She flipped on the lights, illuminating the quiet room. He watched as she peeled off her raincoat and hung it on the back of a chair, and then he did the same with his. They both headed for the coffee pot at the same time.

Drake said, "I'll get it."

To his relief, Maggie consented and turned away. He busied himself making the pot of coffee, trying to ignore her presence in the room. He failed. Her sweet cinnamon scent carried past him as she walked to the refrigerator and pulled out eggs and milk. He dipped his chin and closed his eyes, swearing under his breath. His mind told him he had made the right decision in directing his relationship with Maggie back to a professional level, but at the same time, regret slammed into his heart. How was he supposed to think of her on a professional level when her presence affected him so deeply?

He opened his eyes and found it difficult not to follow her movements as she swept past him and retrieved more items from the pantry. She moved around the kitchen as if she belonged there. His heart lurched in his chest at the thought. He knew she felt at home in Aunt Cammie's kitchen, baking sweet temptations, but would she ever truly feel at home in his wilderness?

The smell of the brewing coffee stirred his stomach, breaking him out of his thoughts. He picked up two mugs and set them on the counter as he waited for the last few drops to perk.

When it finished, he poured the mugs, looked at Maggie and asked, "What do you like in your coffee?"

"Cream."

He put a dab of cream into the mug and offered it to her. She took it and their fingers brushed. He met her eyes, only to find them guarded and wary.

He turned away from her and headed for the bulletin board to update it. He tried to focus, arranging the schedules and posting the relevant information, but his eyes kept trailing back to her. He wondered what she had her hands into this time, when the sweet smells barraged his hungry stomach.

The door in the back opened and Aunt Cammie came shuffling through. "I thought I heard someone rustling 'round in my kitchen." She smiled warmly at Maggie and looked out the dining room window. "I guess we'll be eating indoors this morning."

Maggie released a smile that Drake felt all the way to his core. An unexpected ache coursed through him when he realized how easily she related to Aunt Cammie, and how guarded she was around him. He could only blame himself for the reaction, but it still stung.

Finished with the bulletin board, he took a seat at the long table in the dining room with his back facing Maggie and Aunt Cammie. He studied the lake he knew so well, as the rain fell in heavy drops on its surface. He knew he had gotten himself in too deep with Maggie and wondered if it was already too late for him to resurface with his heart in one piece.

Aunt Cammie asked, "What do think about having waffles this morning?"

Maggie answered, "That sounds great. I'll cut up

the strawberries, add sugar and warm them over the stove for the topping."

"Mmm. Sounds just right to me to brighten up such a dreary morning. Drake, how long's it supposed to rain?" Aunt Cammie added a little louder.

He said, "Throughout the day. It should be clearing overnight."

"That's good. I know you want to make sure the guests get to go on the caving adventure. I'm sure you don't want to delay it for too long."

Drake nodded his head and continued his perusal of the lake. He took a sip of coffee and turned when the front door opened.

Annie and Larry walked in, took off their boots at the door and said a quick greeting to Aunt Cammie and Maggie before heading toward him.

"Good morning Drake," Annie said cheerfully.

"Morning." He offered a smile.

Larry nodded to Drake and seated himself next to his wife. They carried on a trivial conversation while the enticing smells from the kitchen grew stronger.

Drake caught the scent of cinnamon and knew Maggie had come close to him before he even saw her. She reached around and set a plate in front of him with a steaming hot waffle on it and a then placed a bowl of warm strawberries next to it.

"Enjoy," she said as if she were a waitress.

He murmured a word of thanks. Before he knew it, she came back with a tub of butter, a container of warm syrup, silverware and napkins.

The next few minutes went by in a frenzy. Maggie brought Annie and Larry each a hot, fresh waffle. Each time she approached the table, she doused him with a new wave of cinnamon, reminding him of when he held her close and kissed her the night before.

Cyndi and Dillon came inside and joined the

crowd. Before long, three different conversations buzzed around the table, and Drake had to concentrate to keep up with them.

Maggie reached around him again and refreshed his cup of coffee before settling down with the group at the table. The simple, kind gesture chipped a little block from his defenses.

Drake made room for Aunt Cammie at the table when she finally had the time to sit and eat.

"Well, I'd say we've got a bunch of happy campers this morning," Aunt Cammie said as she scooted in next to Drake and dug into her waffle.

Annie said, "This is such a wonderful place for a honeymoon. Away from phones and television. Leaves us more time for..." her face reddened and she giggled.

Larry nudged her and tried to hide his grin.

Cyndi said, "It sure is a nice honeymoon spot. I love the remoteness too. Don't you Dillon?"

He didn't even try to hide his grin as he said, "That's the best part."

Drake noticed Maggie fiddling with her waffle. She had barely touched it and remained quiet amidst all of the chatter around her. Occasionally, she'd smile or add a polite comment, but she remained removed from the rest of the group.

Annie must have noticed because she said, "Maggie, you poor dear. All this talk about newlyweds and happily-ever-afters. I hope it's not bothering you."

Maggie smiled and answered, "Not at all. I'm happy for all of you."

Drake heard the sincerity in her voice, and he knew she meant what she said.

Larry said, "There's no excuse for infidelity, darling. You're better off without him."

"I know I am," Maggie agreed.

Drake saw pain flash across her features before she caught herself and tried to hide it. She diverted her eyes to the lake, watching it as if something important had captured her attention. When she finally looked back to the group, she had regained her composure. Her moistened eyes returned to normal, and she pasted a smile on her lips. No one else at the table seemed to notice. But for him, it was too late. He had seen the pain from what Nathan had done to her. He knew it remained, hidden underneath her smile.

She tugged at his heart again. If she had broken down and run from the room, it wouldn't have affected him as much as seeing her try to hide her emotions. The demure way she collected herself and rejoined the conversation held him captivated.

Nothing he tried to do kept his mind off of her. His eyes drifted to her lips, and he remembered the way they felt, warm and accepting beneath his. He noticed the way the sunlight reflected the highlights in her hair, and the way she tilted her head to the side when she caught him studying her.

Regret slammed into him when her soft eyes met his and became guarded as she straightened in her chair and looked away. He clenched his jaw and wrapped his fingers around his coffee mug and tried to think of ways to make it up to her. He prayed, *Lord, please help me know what to do for Maggie. I don't want her to be hurting. How can I help her?*

Chapter Fifteen

Maggie usually felt cooped up when it rained for too long, but today, she was grateful for the downpour. She needed to spend some time alone. After breakfast, she went back to her cabin, lit the fireplace and settled in for the duration of the rain. She flipped open her book and tried to read, but thoughts of Drake kept creeping in between the lines.

By lunchtime, she had managed to read a few chapters but had no appetite for food. She closed her book and stretched out on the sofa, watching the logs burn to ashes in the fireplace. Had last night's kiss been a mistake? It may have been for Drake but not for her. She closed her eyes and remembered how secure and wanted she had felt in his arms. Too bad the wanted part of it hadn't lasted. Today, she felt completely unwanted.

A knock on the door brought her out of her misery. She climbed from the sofa and made her way to the door. When she opened it, she saw Aunt Cammie on her doorstep, holding a steaming bowl of soup.

Maggie smiled. "Come in."

Rosy cheeked and sopping wet, Aunt Cammie sloshed into the cabin. She handed Maggie the bowl and said, "Eat up now. You need to keep your strength up. Drake's not finished with you yet."

She almost dropped the bowl on the floor. "Not finished with me yet? What do you mean?" Did Aunt Cammie know he had kissed her?

"The caving trip is coming up in a few days. You'll need your strength."

"Oh, that." Maggie released the breath she had been holding. "Please have a seat."

"That cream of broccoli soup should tide you over 'till dinner," Aunt Cammie said as she made her way to the couch and sank into it.

"Thank you so much." Maggie took a sip and sat beside her. "It's delicious."

The warmth soothed her stomach, even though she hadn't felt hungry. "I didn't think you brought lunches out to the guests."

"I usually don't, but for you I made an exception."

"You have a way of making people feel special."

"Thanks. I bet you wish Drake would've learned some of that from me, huh?"

Maggie looked up from her bowl in surprise.

"I told you dear. Not much'll get past me. Think of me as the eyes and ears of this place." She chuckled and added, "Some would say I don't have enough to do. But I tell ya, it's not that. I've got plenty to do. It's just that you can learn a whole lot by listening and observing. Take for example, this morning at breakfast. I saw the tension brewing between you and Drake. Then I saw how he kept his eyes all over you during the meal."

Maggie had noticed that too. He had watched her and she'd had a hard time pretending not to notice.

"Did he tell you what happened?"

"Nope and I'm not going to ask either. I figure it's between you two young folks."

"Okay, but I know you came here to do more than bring me a bowl of soup."

Aunt Cammie nodded. "Okay, I'll admit it. I did."

"What is it? I hope nothing's wrong."

"No dear, nothing's wrong. I came to ask you not to give up on Drake. He's got a stubborn streak that outlasts a whole lot of people. But I detect enough determination in you to know you can handle it."

Maggie shook her head. "I don't want to disappoint you, but he doesn't think I belong here."

"Just don't give up on him, dear. I'll tell you again, he's got a good heart."

"Of gold right?"

She smiled and stood. "Yes. I'd best be getting back before Drake goes and accuses me of meddling again."

"I'd hardly consider helping someone, meddling."

She laughed. "Try to tell Drake that."

Maggie shook her head and laughed with her. She walked Aunt Cammie to the door. "Bye. Thanks again for the soup."

"No problem. Come on by at two o'clock and watch a movie with me. It'll do you some good to get out."

"I'll think about it."

"See you at two then," Aunt Cammie said and shuffled down the porch steps.

Maggie had to smile at the woman's persistence. A movie might not be a bad idea. Maybe she could escape for a few hours and keep her mind focused on something other than Drake.

When two o'clock rolled around, she sloshed through the rain to take Aunt Cammie up on her offer, wondering if she could really keep her mind off of the man for two full hours.

****

Drake knew he'd been had the moment a knock rang out on Aunt Cammie's door. She had invited Maggie to watch the movie too.

"I know what you're doing and it won't work," Drake warned as Aunt Cammie reached for the door.

"Why Drake, I have no idea what you're talking about," she answered innocently as she let Maggie in.

He stretched his arm across the back of the sofa and looked at Maggie's warm smile turn guarded as she noticed him sitting there, occupying a large portion of the sofa. Apparently, she'd been had too.

Drake wondered if she'd take a seat next to him, or scramble to take Aunt Cammie's recliner just to stay away from him. She hesitated in the door for a moment before walking over to the sofa and squeezing herself into the corner farthest away from him.

Aunt Cammie said, "Nothing like a rainy day to cuddle up and watch a romantic movie is there?"

Maggie let out a small cough and wriggled in her seat.

Drake said, "How about an old western instead? Or a sci-fi thriller?" *Anything but romance,* he thought.

Aunt Cammie stretched and yawned saying, "Why don't you two decide, I think I'll go take a nap before preparing dinner, I'm suddenly very tired. I'm making Brunswick stew tonight. I hope you like it Maggie. It's my specialty..." she rattled on, not letting either of them have a chance to protest before she went back to her bedroom and closed the door.

Drake smiled and said, "A little obvious isn't she?"

Maggie nodded and said, "Considering the circumstances...I think I'll just go on back to my cabin and..."

"And leave me with the consequences when Aunt Cammie peeks out here and sees you gone. No way." He shook his head and headed for the DVD collection. "Pick a movie."

After searching through the DVDs, they decided on the least romantic movie they could find, a sci-fi horror one, and settled in. Drake could have kicked himself within ten minutes of the movie's beginning. Maggie's presence kept him so pre-occupied, he had missed the entire plot of the movie. Not wanting to admit he had been distracted, he refused to replay it and catch the lines again.

"Have you seen this one before?" Maggie asked.

"Nope."

"Oh well. I was hoping you'd be able to help me understand it. I'm lost already."

"That makes two of us." He wondered if she had been as distracted as he had been, or if it was just a really bad movie.

Halfway into the film, Drake couldn't help but laugh at the ludicrous special effects and far-fetched storyline. The tension in the room eased perceptibly when Maggie started laughing with him.

She asked, "Do we have to finish this?"

Drake laughed. "I thought you'd never ask." He picked up the remote and flipped the television off. Without the movie playing, he could hear the rumble of Harley's seaplane coming in to land on the lake. "Harley must be bringing Beverly and Stephen back," he commented.

Maggie looked relieved. "I'm so glad Stephen's okay now."

"Me too."

When the room stilled into awkward silence, Drake said, "I'm surprised Aunt Cammie hasn't come out and made sure we're still here. She orchestrated getting us here together really well don't you think?"

"Can't blame her for trying can you?" Maggie asked as she stood from the sofa. "After all, some would think we'd make a good couple."

"Some might think that," he agreed as he climbed from the sofa and met her eyes. When he didn't say anything further, she turned and started for the door.

"What are you going to tell her if she asks how things turned out?" She asked as she reached for the knob.

"I'll tell her…" He lost his train of thought when a loud, crashing sound came from beyond the door to the kitchen. Another one quickly followed along with loud shouts and curses.

Maggie reached to open the door. His protective instincts took immediate control and he yelled, "Don't open it. Let me go first."

She immediately froze in her place and he scooted in front of her.

"Stay back until we know what's happening." He placed a restraining arm in front of her. Satisfied she wouldn't dart out in front of him, he reached for the door, opened it and stepped into a war zone.

****

Maggie peeked around Drake and saw the cause of the chaos. Beverly, armed with a frying pan, chased Stephen around the island in the kitchen. She ranted at him about being thickheaded and flailed the pan in the air as Stephen scrambled around in circles, trying to protect his thick, gel-coated head.

Drake stepped into the kitchen and demanded, "What is going on here?"

Stephen glanced at Drake and earned a sharp clunk on the top of his head for his mistake. Beverly raised the pan to strike again when Drake ran to her and caught it just in time.

He took the pan from Beverly and said in a calm voice, "I don't know what this is about, but I do know that violence is not the answer, Beverly."

Maggie stepped into the kitchen and swept her eyes from Stephen to Beverly. Stephen looked completely dumbfounded, and Beverly looked completely irate.

Stephen rubbed his head in confusion and asked, "What did I say?"

Beverly erupted again. "What did you say? You...you prehistoric caveman! I'll show you..." she reached for another weapon, this time she found a spatula and tried to whack him on the arm with it.

Drake caught her in time, once again, and wrestled the instrument from her.

"Enough!" he shouted.

Beverly turned and paced back and forth across the floor, crossing her arms and mumbling beneath her breath.

Stephen looked at Drake. "Honestly. I don't know what the woman wants from me."

"Humph." Beverly snorted. "You couldn't figure it out if I stamped it across your forehead."

"Stephen, come outside with me." Drake took his arm. He looked at Maggie. "Keep Beverly here for a few minutes."

The kitchen suddenly became quiet. Beverly walked to the large glass windows overlooking the lake and ran shaky hands through her hair.

Maggie walked to the window and noticed the rain had slowed to a light drizzle. Not having a clue as to what to say to the distraught woman she fumbled, "Welcome back."

Beverly looked at her as if she'd lost her mind. After a few more moments of studying the lake, she sighed, "Why can't he just understand what I need?"

Maggie thought for a moment about her own situation with Drake. He knew what she needed, but wasn't willing to relent and give it to her. His acceptance of her meant everything, yet, he held it back out of his own fear.

She returned her focus to Beverly's circumstances. She took a deep breath and asked, "Even if Stephen understood what you need, would he give it to you?"

Beverly shrugged her shoulders and said, "I think so." She tapped her fingers on the windowsill and added, "He does have his good moments. I don't want you to think he's all bad."

Maggie shook her head. "I don't think he's all bad. I've seen him when he's not acting like a total buffoon."

Beverly turned to her and smiled. Then she sighed and explained, "It hasn't always been this way. I have to remind myself what things were like between us at the beginning. They were so good, Maggie. Then? Well…life happens and resentments build up. Before you know it there's a wall up that's nearly impossible to break through. I don't even know if he still loves me."

A jolt went through Maggie. Now she understood the problem. "You say a wall nearly impossible to break through. But nearly means it is still possible, Beverly."

She smiled. "You're a good example for all of us. Do you know that? Your optimism is contagious."

"How can I be a good example when my own life's such a mess?"

She surprised Maggie by placing an arm around her shoulders. "You're a strong woman. You can handle anything that comes your way."

Maggie wasn't so sure about that, but she smiled anyway. She spotted Stephen walking down to the dock just as Drake re-entered the kitchen.

"I'm going to lie down," Beverly said. "Thanks for the talk."

After she left, Maggie turned back to the window and watched Stephen standing on the dock with his head hung low.

Drake came to stand beside her. "That's what resentment will eventually do to a relationship."

Maggie shook her head as a sudden burst of irritation coursed through her. "Well, it hasn't taken years of resentment for me to want to knock you over the head with a frying pan." She ignored the astonished look on his face and walked away.

Men.

Maggie was completely fed up with men in general by the time she reached the dock and approached Stephen. She wanted to lash out at him and tell him exactly what kind of a fool she thought he was acting like.

He turned to her when she came up beside him.

The look of misery on his face took all of the fury out of her, completely deflating her built up anger and leaving her searching for words.

"I've failed her miserably," he said with conviction. "And I don't even know where I went wrong."

Maggie's compassion replaced the remaining irritation she had felt and she reached out, putting a hand on his arm. "How long have you two been married?"

"October twenty-second will be thirty years," Stephen said without hesitation.

"How long have you two been fighting."

"Since...forever." He shook his head. "I don't know." He turned and sat in one of the chairs, motioning her to sit in the other one.

Maggie sat and folded her hands on her lap. She waited for him to offer more information. She didn't have to wait for long.

"I just don't know what to do. I don't know what she wants from me. She won't tell me."

She wondered just how dense the man could get. "Stephen. She wants to know that you love her."

He looked over at her sharply. "She knows I love her." He ran a hand over his slick hair and fidgeted in his chair. "She's my wife."

"Yes, she's your wife, but does she know you love her? How long has it been since you told her?"

"I..." his voice cracked as he looked at her. Maggie saw the moment he recognized the truth. "Oh no. Could it be that simple?"

Maggie nodded. "It may not be the answer to all of your problems. But I'd say it's a pretty good place to start."

He looked out at the water and Maggie took a moment to study him. Dark circles showed some of the strain he had been under, and his red-rimmed eyes showed fatigue.

"When the snake bit me, I had no idea she would

react the way she did. I think she still loves me, too."

"I do too, Stephen. I saw the terror in her eyes when she thought she might lose you."

"I guess sometimes it takes a crisis to show how someone really feels about you."

Maggie nodded in agreement. "Yeah. It's a shame it has to come down to that isn't it? I think everyone takes someone in their life for granted. Most times, they don't realize it until it's too late."

Stephen looked over at her and smiled. "You know you're not half bad."

"Excuse me?"

"There is more to you than your looks."

"Gee. Thanks. I think." Maggie tried hard to control her sudden annoyance.

He looked over his shoulder. "Drake's watching us. I'd better go before he comes over and wrestles me to the dock like he did to your ex-fiancé."

"How did you know about that? You weren't even here."

"Word travels fast in a small resort, remember?"

Maggie smiled. "Ah. Yes, I remember."

Stephen took a step then hesitated. "Do you really think it'll help?"

"What will help?"

"Telling her I love her."

"If it's true. Yes."

He nodded. "Of course it's true. She's my life." Stephen walked away with a renewed hope evident in his eyes.

Maggie said a quick prayer for Stephen and Beverly as she headed toward the shore. She carefully avoided Drake's probing stare from inside Aunt Cammie's dining room as she made her way back to her cabin.

Chapter Sixteen

The sun came out the next day, bright and cheery. Maggie rose from the bed with reluctance, then flopped back into it, reminding herself she was on vacation. She fell asleep again and slept until she couldn't sleep anymore, and then took a long soak in the Jacuzzi.

She emerged from her cabin during the day, only to eat. She spent the rest of the day lounging around reading, re-organizing her backpack and rearranging her clothes. She was a little embarrassed at herself for threatening Drake with a frying pan and wasn't too anxious to face him again. Thankfully, he hadn't been around when she had ventured out to eat.

Finally, as the day turned into night, she decided to join the others at the campfire, knowing she couldn't avoid the man for the rest of her stay here.

She hadn't realized how late it had become until she approached the campfire and noticed that Stephen, Beverly, Annie and Larry had already retired for the evening and Cyndi and Dillon stood, preparing to leave.

She prayed she could handle being alone with Drake as she settled into a lounge chair. She avoided eye contact with him as she said goodnight to Cyndi and Dillon. When only the two of them were left, she had no choice but to look at him. He held a stick in his hand and used a knife to shave the end into a point, carving it into a new marshmallow stick. She saw a pile of them next to his chair.

"I wouldn't really come after you with a frying

pan. You know that right?"

Drake smiled and looked up from the sticks. "I'd like to see you try..." he said with challenge in his eyes. "I could take you." As soon as he said the words, his eyes deepened and he returned his focus to the stick.

Suddenly, the fire seemed much hotter as her face flushed. She hurriedly tried to change the subject. "Seems like you're always busy doing something."

"Seems that way because I am." He flipped the knife closed, picked up the pile of sticks and met her eyes.

The sight of him carving the marshmallow sticks made her curiosity peak. "Did you carve the rocking chairs on the porches?"

Drake lifted his chin and laughed. "No. What gave you that idea?"

Suddenly embarrassed she tapped her fingers on her knees and shrugged. "You look capable enough."

"Do I?" He quickly sobered and his blue eyes intensified. "Thanks for the vote of confidence, but it's not my specialty. Carving marshmallow sticks is a little easier than carving a rocker." He set the pile of sticks down next to his feet before saying, "But I would like to try something like that one day. I'm planning on clearing a space in the woods over there." He pointed to an area behind him. "And building a workshop. Maybe I'll try it sometime. Who knows?"

"You'd be good at it."

"What makes you think that?"

"You have the patience for it."

Drake leaned forward and placed his elbows on his knees. He looked at her through the swirling campfire smoke and said, "It takes more than patience to create something so beautiful."

His eyes roamed over her, she warmed and felt as if he were talking about her. "Yes. I suppose it does," she answered softly.

Drake hesitated before saying, "Maggie. I shouldn't have…"

She held up a hand. "It's okay. You already said you shouldn't have kissed me."

"I was going to say I shouldn't have hurt you like I did the other night. I'm sorry."

Maggie managed a weak smile. "I know you didn't mean to."

He nodded, picked up the fresh sticks and left without another word.

A strong surge of loneliness replaced the warmth she had felt in Drake's presence. She curled onto her side and watched the flames from the fire, wondering how she would survive the second week at Drake's Retreat with her heart intact.

****

Drake never lost sight of her. He stayed in the shadows, his heart warring with his mind.

He needed to go to his cabin and catch up on some paperwork, but when he turned and saw her curl up on the lounge chair with sadness in her eyes, he couldn't bring himself to leave her there alone.

He stood still for some time, watching her. He thought of the pain he had caused her, on top of what she had already been through. Guilt stabbed at him again. He knew he had no right to want her. But no matter how much he told himself that, he still did.

When she drifted off to sleep, he went back to the campfire and poured a bucket of water on it, causing steam to explode from the dying embers. Maggie shifted on the lounge chair and he went to her. He placed one arm under her knees, the other around her shoulders, and lifted her into his arms.

She stirred slightly when he pulled her to his chest. Warmth shot through his veins as she placed her palm on his shoulder and tucked her head under his neck.

Then she stiffened as she came to a fuller awareness.

"Drake, I can walk," she said in a groggy voice and arched her back, trying to get out of his grasp.

"Shh. I've got you." He held her tighter.

She relaxed and let him carry her. He liked the feel of her in his arms. She was no burden for his strength, and he carried her with ease. As he walked, he kept telling himself to put her down and to walk away from her. But he couldn't resist taking her all the way to her door.

"I didn't mean to fall asleep. How long was I out?"

Drake gently set her on her feet and answered, "Only for a few minutes."

"Thanks for not leaving me out there for the bears to snack on."

He laughed and said, "No way would I let that happen."

She tilted her head to the side and peered up at him. "You know you don't have to feel responsible for me."

"I always look out for my guests' needs," he said. It was only after he'd spoken those words aloud that he knew what he could do to help her. As the idea came to him, he mentally kicked himself for not thinking about it before. "There's a place I want to take you to tomorrow. Be ready to take a ride right after breakfast."

"A ride? Where to?" Her eyebrows rose.

"I'll tell you when we get there." He spun around and headed down the steps.

"Can you give me a hint?"

At the bottom step he paused and said, "It's a place that will help you find your way."

He walked away with a satisfied smile playing on his lips.

****

Maggie arrived at breakfast the next morning

with jittery nerves. She tapped her toes on the ground under the picnic table, curious as to where Drake planned on taking her this morning. She told herself her anticipation had nothing to do with being alone with him again, but she knew better. As much as she tried to think of him as only her host for the duration of her stay here, she came up short. Her attraction to him could not be denied, no matter how hard she tried.

She had seen his compassion and experienced his kindness. She'd even glimpsed his heart of gold that Aunt Cammie had told her about, and it left her wanting to see more of it.

"Good morning." Drake's deep voice vibrated through her raw nerves as he walked up behind her.

She smiled and clasped her hands together. "Morning." She noticed a smile tug on his lips as he sat down across from her. They were the first two to arrive at the table, and Maggie took the opportunity to ask him, "Will you tell me where we're going?"

He shook his head. "You'll see."

"Just tell me we won't be taking the ride in the seaplane..."

His smile brightened. "No seaplane today. We'll go in my truck."

"Your truck? What truck?"

"I've got a pick-up I park a little ways down the road."

"Why do you park it down the road? Are you trying to hide it?"

He shrugged. "Having a truck in view of the guests takes away from the sense of remoteness, don't you think?"

"I can see that. Good idea."

Drake smiled. "I thought so too." He looked up past her shoulder and said, "Good morning Annie."

The rest of the guests came trickling in for breakfast a few at a time. The whole time Maggie ate, she wondered where Drake planned to take her.

He didn't give her any hints during breakfast, even though she tried to wrangle some out of him.

After breakfast, they walked down the road behind Aunt Cammie's Kitchen. As they rounded a curve, a full-sized silver truck came into view along with a forest green SUV.

"I assume the SUV is Aunt Cammie's?"

"Sure is." Drake walked to the passenger door of the truck and opened it for her, giving her a slight nod as she entered the truck. He shut the door, leaving her alone with his spicy scent which lingered in the clean interior.

She took a moment to appreciate his freshly shaven jaw and clean, crisp looking shirt as he rounded the truck in front of her. She also noticed he wore jeans that looked almost brand new. The combination made her feel like they were going on a casual date.

She sat quietly as he revved the engine and started driving down the narrow, dusty gravel road. To her surprise, after traveling downhill for a few miles, Drake turned onto another road and headed back up the mountain in a different direction.

"You've got me really curious now," she said then looked out the window, over the side of the narrow road. She could only see the tops of trees a few feet from the road, making her stomach plunge to her toes.

"The truck has four-wheel drive, and I'm used to driving this road. I'll be sure you arrive safely," Drake said as if reading her thoughts.

She looked down at her white knuckles as she gripped the door handle and let out a breath. "You noticed."

He glanced her way and grinned. "It would be hard not to."

Maggie watched him handle the wheel with confidence. He looked more than competent enough to drive them safely over the twists and turns of the mountains. She began to relax as they continued on their way.

"We're almost there."

After traversing a series of hairpin turns, Drake drove into a clearing. Maggie immediately spotted a fairly small, white clapboard church. Stained glass windows decorated the well-kept building and a steeple stood high overhead.

"You're taking me to church? I forgot it was Sunday." Maggie gasped as she looked down at her jeans. "I'm not dressed appropriately."

"You're fine. This is a community based church, people come as they are." Drake pointed to some people entering the church. "Look at them."

She looked at what the people wore. Most dressed in jeans, some dressed in khakis. All of the church-goers wore casual clothes.

"Oh, okay." She felt a little better.

"I think you'll like it here."

"Do you come here often?"

"As often as I can." He stepped outside and opened the door for her before she reached the handle.

He held his hand out to her and helped her ease from the oversized vehicle. She tugged her shirt down and ran a hand through her hair.

"You look beautiful."

Maggie's breath caught and her chest tightened as she quickly turned to him. "Thank you."

"You're welcome."

As they walked into the church Maggie asked, "Do you bring many of your guests here?"

"No. None before you."

"Why do I get the special privilege?"

He hesitated in his answer, and before he could speak an older couple approached them. He introduced Maggie to them, along with several of the other members of the church. The service began before she could ask him again why he'd brought her here.

A sense of peace came over her as a band came onto the stage and began playing a modern Christian song. She stood along with Drake and sang along the best she could. She tuned in to Drake's deep, downright sexy voice as he sang the words. A blush rose to her cheeks at the thoughts she had and she tried to focus on something other than the vibrant man standing next to her.

When the pastor led the congregation in prayer, Maggie bend her head and peeked to the side. Nothing she had seen or experienced before prepared her for the impact at seeing Drake sitting with his head bowed and his hands clasped in front of him in prayer. It took all of her willpower not to reach over and lay her hand on his.

She thought back to the first time she had seen Drake at the check-in-center. Never in a million years would she have guessed she would be sitting in church next to him a week later, watching him pray, and falling in love with him.

She sucked in a breath when the realization struck her. Drake must have heard her. He reached over and squeezed her hand. He smiled at her before settling in for the duration of the sermon.

The pastor held her attention for the remainder of the hour. He spoke of the Scriptures in terms that she related to in her everyday life, and she soaked in the wisdom of his words. Before she knew it, the pastor had finished the sermon. She turned and saw Drake watching her with an endearing smile on his face.

He stood and placed a hand on her lower back, applying gentle pressure as they left the building. Maggie enjoyed the warmth of his touch and missed it when he removed his hand.

Once outside Maggie asked again, "Why did you bring me here?"

He hesitated, looking at the tree branches

swaying in the breeze overhead. Then he looked at her. "Because I knew you were still having a hard time dealing with what happened with Nathan. And, because I felt God leading me to bring you here."

"Did you know what the sermon was going to be about?" she asked as they slowly made their way back to the truck.

"No." He shook his head. "Why?"

"Because I felt like God was speaking directly to me through the pastor. Does that ever happen to you?"

"Every time I come here. I guess when a church is the right fit that's how you're supposed to feel."

"Then this church must fit me perfectly."

Pleasure flashed across his eyes. "I'm glad you liked it."

They walked side by side to his truck and Maggie leaned against the passenger side door, putting her hands into her pockets. "There's something I still don't understand."

"What don't you understand?" Drake's expression became serious, as he leaned his shoulder on the truck right beside her.

"The pastor mentioned that we're children of God, and He loves us more than we can even imagine. If God loves me so much, then why did he let me get hurt so bad? He could have stopped it. He could have prevented the whole thing from happening."

"Yes, He could have," Drake agreed.

"But He didn't. Why?"

"Only God knows the reasons for the things that happen." Drake lifted a hand and brushed a strand of hair from her face with his fingertips. "He knows and understands everything, and He has a much broader perspective than we do. He lets us go through pain for a reason, Maggie. We may not understand why at the time, but I know He has a plan, and I know He makes good things come from bad situations."

She stared at him for a moment before answering, "I never thought of it that way."

"I believe one day you'll understand. One day we'll all understand. Until then? We have to keep trusting Him and having faith that He'll always be there with us."

"I know one good thing that came out of the situation."

"What's that?" He sent her a searching look.

"I met you."

His eyes widened, and then lowered to her lips. He whispered, "Maggie…"

She stood still and continued, "You've led me back to God each time we've discussed something really important. You've shown me that I need to make God the center of my life, to lean on Him and trust Him no matter what happens. For that, I'll always be grateful to you."

He nodded slowly. His eyes lifted to hers and he cleared his throat. "I'm glad I could help."

"Thanks for bringing me here."

He reached around her to open the door. "No problem."

Chapter Seventeen

Maggie finished her book early Sunday afternoon and sat on the rocker, looking out at the lake. She wished she had brought more than one novel with her, and she chewed on her lip, wondering what to do next. She thought about baking something or taking a nap. Finally, she decided to take a walk around the resort and see what kind of trouble she could get into.

She took her time, looking around the area and enjoying the sounds of nature. As she came up to the main area of camp, she noticed the storage shed's door had been left open. She peeked inside and found a stack of fishing poles, tackle boxes, a few oars and a pile of life preservers.

Fishing sounded like a great idea on a lazy Sunday afternoon, so she quickly picked out a rod and rooted around in a tackle box for a fresh hook. When she had everything she needed, she shut the door and made her way to the shoreline.

Annie and Larry lounged on the dock and she didn't want to disturb them, so she headed down the shoreline back toward her cabin. She passed by it and made her way through the forest toward the other side of the lake.

She stopped and shuffled her feet around looking under leaves. "Bingo," she said to herself when she found a few worms squirming on the fresh earth. She scooped one up and hooked it, then searched for a place to cast her line.

Before she knew it, she had traveled to the far side of the lake. Deciding she had gone far enough, she stopped and found a solid, flat rock to sit on. She cast her line into the water and waited, watching the water gently lap the rocky shore and letting the warm afternoon sunshine filter through the trees and warm her back.

A sudden tug on the line had her jumping to her feet and she gave an involuntary yelp. Finally remembering to jerk back on the line, she hooked the fish and reeled it in.

"Aren't you a cute little thing?" she asked the embarrassingly little, small-mouthed bass as she drew it from the water. If her brothers had seen her catch such a tiny thing, they never would have let her forget it.

She took hold of the fish by the mouth and removed the hook. "Off you go. You need to grow a few more years before you let yourself get caught again." She let the little guy swim away and hoped another bigger fish wouldn't come and scoop it up for lunch.

"Do you always talk to the fish you catch?" Drake's deep voice came from behind her.

She whipped around, nearly hooking herself in the thumb, and saw Drake leaning against a nearby tree. He stood with his arms and ankles crossed, as if he'd been watching her the whole time.

Her face heated. "Only when I think I'm alone."

Drake stood from the tree and ambled over to her. He looked at the empty hook. "I don't have any live bait. What did you use?"

"A worm. She scooted more leaves over. "See. There are tons of them."

He looked at her quizzically. "*You* touch worms?"

Maggie gave an exasperated sigh. "Yes. A city girl touched and hooked a worm. Imagine the headlines…"

He gave a deep, lighthearted chuckle and shook his head. "You never cease to amaze me."

"I have four brothers."

"Ah," he said as if that explained everything.

"So what are you doing out here?"

"I'm working on another hiking trail."

She lifted her eyebrows and her mouth dropped open. "You clear the hiking trails?"

He shrugged. "Who else?"

The rod began to slip from her fingers and Drake reached out to catch it, keeping it from falling to the ground.

"Even the eight mile one?"

"Yeah. It's a lot of work, but someone has to do it."

"I just assumed you had a crew come in and clear the paths for you."

"Now what fun would that be?" He smiled. "Come on. I'll show you."

Maggie began walking beside him. "I guess I'm as surprised to find out you personally clear the trails as you are that I touched a worm."

He broke out into laughter. "I guess so."

When his dimple appeared and tingles of warmth shot through her spine, she knew she had completely fallen in love with this lumberjack of a man. She had felt it happen at church, now she felt it again. He had hooked her for sure. She caught him studying her, and she quickly looked away.

"I haven't changed my mind Maggie," he said as if he had read her thoughts.

Remorse coursed through her. He still didn't think she belonged here. Even after discovering she touched worms. What more did the man want? She felt like she was climbing up a mountain too steep to traverse when it came to Drake Strong.

She remained silent as she walked along beside him. They soon came to a path that paralleled a wide stream.

"This is a little steeper than the other trails I've opened up. That's why I saved it to work on until I completed the other ones," he said as he set the fishing pole at the base of the trail and headed up.

As they climbed the steep terrain, Drake reached back and took her hand, helping her along the rougher stretches.

"I'll smooth the trail out more after I finish clearing the main obstacles."

"It's not so bad," she said through her heavy breathing.

He slowed his pace as they came to the end of the trail. "This is where it ends for now. It'll go another two miles up to a scenic viewing area when I'm finished."

Maggie looked farther up the mountain. The trees and undergrowth that Drake had yet to clear dumbfounded her. "Have all the trails been this difficult to clear?"

"Not all of them." He shook his head. "I was able to follow deer paths for a few miles on some of them. That helped a lot."

She looked down and spotted a bush small enough to pull out by hand. She reached down and grabbed it by the roots. She pulled and twisted it until it gave up and tore from the ground.

"What are you doing?"

"I'm helping you," Maggie answered as she reached for a rock and pulled it out of the path.

"I didn't bring you here to coerce you into helping me. You don't have to..."

"I know. But I want to."

He shook his head. "Okay." He sat on a rock and watched her work.

"Are you going to help or just sit there and watch me?" she asked after breaking a sweat.

"It's kinda fun seeing you struggle to prove yourself to me."

She stopped instantly and turned to face him. She swiped her brow with her forearm. "Prove myself to you? Drake I'm moving rocks. What's that supposed to prove?"

"I don't know. You tell me."

Exasperated she lifted her hands high in the air. "You are a difficult man, Drake Strong."

She abandoned her work on the trail and started walking down the steep terrain.

"Look out for that..." Drake began to say, but before he could finish Maggie slipped and fell on her rear. "Wet spot," he finished with a chuckle.

"I'm so glad I could help entertain you," she said with mud coated hands and a sore tailbone.

"I'm sorry. Let me help you." He snickered one more time before coming to her side and pulling her to her feet.

"Oh, so now you're a gentleman."

"I wouldn't want to disappoint you."

"For the record, knights in shining armor never laugh at damsels in distress."

He immediately sobered. "I'm not one of the heroes you read about in your romance novels, Maggie."

She let out a sharp laugh and dusted off her jeans. "I'd be the first to agree with you on that point."

"You didn't have to agree so quickly did you?"

Grinning, Maggie shrugged her shoulders and continued down the hill without answering.

****

Drake followed her footsteps, a little sore that she had so quickly discounted the notion of him being a knight in shining armor. He wondered if he could fill that role in her life, then quickly shook his head. Not even real knights lived up to that standard.

He smirked when he noticed the smudge of dirt left on Maggie's rear. When he caught himself watching a little too closely, he stepped to the side and came up beside her on the trail. He needed to keep his mind somewhere else so he searched for something to talk about.

"Cyndi and Dillon are the only guests that want to try the caving trip the day after tomorrow. That means you can stay at the cabins if you want to."

"I'm going," she answered immediately.

"Are you sure? You don't have to, Maggie."

"I'm sure," she said with a hint of annoyance.

"It's a few miles to the entrance of the cave. Once we get there we'll be inside for most of the day." He glanced at her and added, "Be prepared for rats and snakes near the entrance. There'll be a few bats along the way too."

"Are you trying to talk me out of it?"

"No, just preparing you for the possibilities."

"Thanks for the warning," she spoke with a touch of sarcasm.

Maggie kept the chip on her shoulder the rest of the way down the trail. Drake ground his teeth together in frustration. How could he be so at ease with her one moment and so at odds with her the next?

Chapter Eighteen

The mouth of the cave looked more like a crack in the rock than an entrance to an underground cavern. If Maggie had been looking for it by herself, she would have walked right past it.

Drake turned to face them and instructed, "Turn on your headlamps and keep your spare flashlight with you. Leave your backpacks outside. We'll be going into some tight spaces, so there will be no room for them."

Maggie set her pack down, pulled out her gloves and put them on. She turned on the headlamp and took a drink from her water bottle before returning it to her pack.

Cyndi and Dillon adjusted their gear as Drake waited patiently for them all to get ready.

"Let's go," Dillon said, anxiously.

Drake led the way into the dark crevice between the rocks. She watched as he disappeared first, then Dillon, and finally Cyndi. She bent down to scoot inside and stepped into the abyss.

Light filtered into the cave from the opening, and Maggie saw the outline of the large room they stood in. "Looks like a bear cave."

Drake chuckled. "I've run into a bear here a time or two. I haven't seen one near here in a few months though."

Goose bumps traveled down her arms as she wondered if a bear would come and claim the cave as his dwelling before they exited the cavern.

As they made their way deeper into the cave, the sounds from the forest dulled, then became obsolete. Maggie listened to her boots crunch on the rocky terrain and echo across the surrounding walls. Soon, the light from the entrance became a distant memory, and shadows loomed in every corner and crevice. She heard a bat squeak and automatically jumped, ducking her head.

"Maggie, are you okay?" The concern in Drake's voice sounded genuine as he stopped and looked at her.

"Yes." She nodded, pleased to discover she meant it. Maybe her range of fears didn't include small, dark spaces after all. Even the bat didn't freak her out like she thought it would.

Drake held his hand out to her. "Come up here behind me. Dillon and Cyndi can follow you."

She leaned down under the low ceiling, passed in front of the newlyweds and took his hand. Immediately comforted by his strong grasp, she looked into his eyes and murmured, "Thanks."

He nodded. "We'll have to crawl on our knees from here and then go to our stomachs for a few feet before the cave opens up again." He looked at Maggie, Dillon then Cyndi. "Everyone okay?"

"Yes," they all answered in unison.

Drake let Maggie out of his grasp and dropped to his knees. Dust flew through the dank air as they all shuffled along behind him. The ceiling dipped lower and lower, until they finally had to drop to their stomach and squiggle through the passageway. The air felt cooler and cooler the deeper they crawled and the natural scent of the earth became stronger.

Drake suddenly disappeared in front of Maggie and she held her breath. A second later, she saw his hand reach out in front of her. She grabbed for him, the contact instantly dissolving the fear that began to seep into her when she lost sight of him. He used his strength to help pull her the rest of the way through the opening.

She stood, noticing the dusty ground had turned into wet, sticky clay under her boots. She took a step to the side and looked up. Awe filled her at the chasm that awakened before her. The rays of light from her headlamp illuminated stalactites and stalagmites adorning the top and bottom of the large chamber. Dozens of them sprouted from the earth, thousands of years in the making.

"Wow! This is incredible."

Dillon crawled out into the opening and grabbed for Cyndi's wrist.

Cyndi asked, "What? What's so wow, Maggie?"

"Come and look." She smiled as Cyndi bounced up into Dillon's arms.

"Way cool!" Cyndi exclaimed.

"Wait until you see the next large chamber," Drake announced. "It's not far from here, but we'll have to get over the chasm first."

"Chasm?" Maggie asked, her fears taking immediate control over her.

"Look down," Drake said simply.

She did. Only then did she realize she stood on a three foot ledge. She peered over the edge into the darkness and the rays from her headlamp didn't reach the bottom.

"H-How deep is it?"

Drake answered, "Fifty-seven feet."

"How do we get across it?"

"We jump."

"Jump?" Maggie's head started to swim.

"It's only a few feet across to the other side. It'll be okay. I've never had anyone fall." Drake looked down and added, "Yet."

She backed up as far as she could from the edge and pressed against the rock. "You said there might be snakes."

"There might be."

"And rats."

"True."

"And bats."

"Yes."

"You didn't mention jumping over bottomless chasms."

"It's not bottomless." Drake dropped a rock into the dark hole. It eventually clinked at the bottom. "See."

Maggie began to shake her head.

Drake stepped in front of her with his back to the edge. "Look at me Maggie."

She looked up into the shadows of his face, taking care not to shine her headlamp in his eyes.

"I know you can do this. Otherwise, I wouldn't have let you come with us."

She thought about it for a moment and answered, "I guess if I can climb up a mountain, ride down a zip line and face an arrogant ex-fiancé, I can do this right?"

"Right." He nodded. "Just don't think about how far down it is."

Dillon asked, "Mind if we go on ahead?"

"That's fine." Drake turned halfway around to look at him. "There's only one way into the largest chamber. Stop there and wait for us."

"Good deal." Dillon announced and leapt over the chasm with ease. Cyndi jumped immediately into Dillon's waiting arms.

Cyndi called out, "It's easy Maggie. Don't worry. You can do it."

After some scuffling and maneuvering, Cyndi and Dillon headed around the corner and disappeared from sight.

Drake turned to Maggie. "I'll go first. Then you can leap across and into my arms, like Cyndi just did with Dillon."

Jumping into Drake's arms hardly seemed like keeping things professional between them, but given the circumstances, pointing it out to him didn't seem feasible.

"Okay."

Drake reached out to her and gave her hand a

quick, reassuring squeeze before turning and leaping over the hole.

"You make it look so easy."

"It's not hard if you're not afraid of heights."

"I told you before, I'm not afraid of heights. I'm only afraid of falling."

His deep chuckle vibrated across the chamber. "If you say so." He positioned himself against the far wall and held his arms out. "Come to me, Maggie."

Her eyes jerked to his. "You really think I can do this?"

"Have confidence in yourself. I do."

She sucked in a breath. "You do?"

Their eyes met and locked. "Yes." Drake's voice lowered. "I do."

Maggie stepped closer to the edge, said a quick prayer and started to jump. Then she stopped at the last second, her fear holding her back.

"Don't hesitate Maggie. That'll only get you hurt."

Maggie peeked over the edge again.

"Don't look down. Look into my eyes."

Maggie looked at him. "Why are you doing this for me? You could just leave me here."

"No. I'm not giving up on you. And I'm not letting you give up on yourself. Come on, baby. Jump."

His use of the word 'baby' caught her off guard. From the surprised look on his face, Maggie knew he hadn't planned on saying it.

Her pulse jumped and she took advantage of the quick surge of adrenaline that coursed through her by taking a step back, then leaping toward Drake. She landed straight into his arms and slammed against his chest. He wrapped his arms around her immediately and held her close.

"You did it!"

"I did, didn't I?" Maggie laughed in relief. Her breath caught in her throat when she lifted her face to look at him. Attraction, clear and strong struck her, settling deep into her heart.

"You're doing it again."

"Doing what again?"

"Biting your lower lip."

"Oh." Maggie released her lip and started to back away. "Sorry."

"Don't be sorry. I have to be honest with you. I don't mind it so much when you do that."

She watched as his eyes traveled to her lips again. She caught a flash of desire in his gaze before he suddenly released her.

"Let's catch up," he said a little gruffly as he turned away.

To Maggie's surprise and relief, Drake took her hand in his again as they traversed the passageway leading to the next chamber. She felt comforted by the touch of his hand, even through the gloves they both wore.

They walked through the tall passageway without having to lean over or crawl. One spot became narrow, but Drake helped her slide through it.

Maggie tugged Drake to a stop and looked up. "It looks like we're in a crack in the earth."

"We are."

"I never saw anything like this when I visited a commercial cave."

"They won't let you in the smaller areas of those caves. This is a totally different experience isn't it?"

"Yeah. I'm surprised it doesn't scare me."

"You're stronger and braver than you give yourself credit for."

"I..." Maggie started to argue but lost her breath when his words soaked in.

"Don't deny it. Nathan took a lot from you. It's time you take it back."

His words shot straight to her soul and a new understanding bombarded her. She dug her feet into the sticky clay, refusing to move when Drake began to walk again. "You're right. It is time."

He smiled, producing his irresistible dimple. Maggie leaned over and placed a kiss on it, before she had time to think it through.

Heat rose up her neck. "Oh. I guess I shouldn't have done that either. Sorry again."

"Don't be sorry," he said in a low whisper. His eyes trailed over her face and landed on her lips. He bent his neck and brought his lips close to hers.

Maggie put a hand up to his chest. "I don't want you to have any more regrets." But as she said the words, she leaned in closer to him, willing him to continue toward her.

"I won't regret this." He bent his head further and his lips claimed hers with a possessiveness that both surprised and excited her. He captured her waist with his arm, pulling her close and splaying his hand across her lower back.

His kiss sent a new wave of conflicting emotions within her. When he pulled away she asked, "You're confusing me Drake. What do you really want?"

A muscle in his jaw twitched. "I want you to be happy. I want to help you heal."

"You have helped me. You've always pointed me to the Lord for all of my needs. When I needed confidence, you pointed me to Him. When I needed to know which direction to go, you pointed me to Him. I believe He put you into my life to help me realize these things. You've helped me more than you can imagine. I feel so much more confident in myself now. After facing my fears and riding down the zip line and facing Nathan..." she took a deep breath and looked up above her head then continued, "then crawling around in these dark, tight spaces I feel like I can do so much more than I ever thought I could. I think I'm going to be okay, Drake."

"I know you are."

She looked at him and asked seriously, "Do you believe God led me here?"

He slowly nodded his head. "Yes I do."

"Do you believe He could have plans for me to stay? For me to belong here?" Maggie asked with a tremble in her voice. She needed for him to say yes. She needed for him to accept her. She needed for him to tell her, *you belong here.* She held her breath, waiting for an answer that didn't come.

He started to speak then stopped, shrugged and cleared his throat before looking away. "We should catch up to Dillon and Cyndi. They're probably wondering where we are."

Disappointment ran through Maggie and she ducked her head, not wanting Drake to catch the tears welling up in her eyes. She brushed a clump of mud from her jeans with shaky fingers and said, "You first."

They traveled the rest of the way to the larger room in silence. Maggie heard the pounding of her saddened heart and her boots sticking to the wet, mucky ground as she trudged along behind Drake. When they caught up with Dillon and Cyndi in the larger chamber, Maggie changed her focus from the man traveling in front of her to the fascinating room that opened up before them.

Several large columns of joined stalactites and stalagmites lived in the room. From the look of the moisture still on them, Maggie assumed they still continued to grow. She noticed a pristine pool of water that lay so still the surrounding formations reflected perfectly in its glasslike appearance. She knelt next to the pool of water. Unable to resist, she removed the gloves from her hands and dipped a finger into the cold, shallow water. The resulting ripples disrupted the clear reflection, making the formations look distorted and confused, in direct resemblance of how she felt inside.

The moment she thought her life had gotten on

track again, she found herself, her happiness too dependent upon a person again. She couldn't allow that to happen. She refused to allow that to happen. If Drake didn't accept her being here, she'd have to accept his decision and live with it, no matter how it tore her heart in two.

Cyndi came to kneel beside her. "Are you okay? You look so deep in thought."

Maggie forced a smile. "Yes, I'm okay."

"It's amazing in here isn't it?"

"I'll never stop being amazed at God's wonderful creations."

"I hear ya," Cyndi agreed and moved back to her husband's side.

After they spent several minutes admiring the chamber, Drake took a step toward Maggie and held out his gloved hand. "We'd better head back to the entrance. I want to make sure we get back to the cabins before nightfall."

Maggie took his hand and he lifted her up. When he didn't release her from his grasp, she met his eyes.

He whispered, "Maggie…"

She quickly held up a hand to halt his words. "Don't worry Drake. If you still don't think I belong here when the two weeks are over, I'll leave." Her heartbeat intensified as she gathered enough courage to add, "But it's only fair for you to know that I've fallen in love with you, and I think I…" she paused and took a breath, "I know…I could be happy here, in your wilderness with you." She held her breath, hoping she wouldn't regret her impulsive admission.

A flicker of hope flashed in his eyes before they became guarded again. He released her hand but held her eyes captive with his steady stare as he said, "You might think you like it here enough to stay Maggie, but what happens when the seasons change? What happens when the winter comes and the isolation becomes unbearable? You asked me if I felt isolated out here. How would you really feel after weeks of bitter coldness and harsh conditions? Even Aunt Cammie heads south in the coldest months." He held up a hand when she started to speak. "It's better if we don't fool ourselves into thinking this could work Maggie. I couldn't bear to have you resent me if I asked you to stay and sometime later you realize you couldn't handle living here."

"It sounds like you have your mind made up."

He looked away and adjusted his headlamp, shuffled his boots and repositioned his gloves before looking back at her. Finally, he took a deep breath. "It's best this way."

"Is it Drake?" She took a step away from him. "Is it best this way or is it just safer for you to hide in your wilderness alone? Is it just safer to not take a risk on loving someone again?" She didn't wait for an answer as she turned and followed Cyndi and Dillon back through the narrow passageway.

Chapter Nineteen

In the few days that followed the caving trip,
Maggie perfected the art of relaxing. She allowed
herself extra rest to help heal the sore muscles she
had acquired inside the cave. The bruises she had
along her shins and arms from crawling around on
the rocky cave floor had already begun to fade away.

On the few occasions that their paths crossed,
Drake had been polite to her, yet cautious at the
same time. He had pulled away from her, and it hurt
her more than she cared to admit.

On the last full day of her stay at Drake's
Retreat, she woke early and made her way straight
to the Jacuzzi tub, turned on the faucets and climbed
in. She knew the hot water and bubbling jets might
ease her body, but they couldn't even begin to sooth
the soreness in her heart.

She soaked in the tub for a while, trying to keep
her mind off of Drake. She failed miserably. Every
time she tried to focus on something other than him,
her thoughts made their way back on their own.

A brisk knock on the door brought her up and
out of the tub instantly. She grabbed the robe and
tucked it around her waist as she walked to the door
and opened it.

"What did you say to Stephen?" Drake asked
abruptly as he leaned against the door jamb.

Goose bumps traveled down her arms and legs
at his rushed words and her eyes widened. "What do
you mean?"

"The other night on the dock...what did you
say?"

"Why? What's wrong?" Her eyebrows drew

together in concern as wariness crept up her spine.

"I want to know Maggie," he said, crossing his arms in front of his chest.

"I told him to tell Beverly he loved her."

Drake raised his eyebrows. "That's it?"

"Mostly. You're scaring me Drake. What happened?"

"Stephen and Beverly are at the breakfast table."

"Is that a bad thing?"

He smiled and shook his head. "They're being nice to each other. They're also sitting side by side, and they even kissed once."

A smile exploded from Maggie, and she broke into deep laughter. Relief spread into her, "I thought you were going to tell me they were getting a divorce."

"No. They're acting like...well, like they love each other."

"That's because they do." Maggie let out the breath she'd been holding.

Drake stood still for few moments before saying, "You just saved their marriage."

She shook her head. "No I didn't. I just..."

"You did, Maggie." He released his arms and took a step toward her, crossing the threshold into her cabin. "You cared enough to reach out to them. You saw what they needed and pointed it out."

"It's what anyone would have done..."

"No, it's not. Everyone didn't do it. You did it Maggie." He smiled. "You're amazing, you know that?"

"Amazing enough to save a marriage but not enough to fit into your wilderness?"

His lips tightened, his jaw clenched and he stood taller. "Maggie..."

"I'm sorry you can't see that I belong here when I'm telling you straight from my heart that I feel like I do. I feel like God led me here for a reason. Are you discounting that?"

"Not at all." Drake shook his head. "You've changed since you came here. You've begun to heal and you have your confidence back. Maybe that's why He led you here."

"I believe that's a big part of it, but not the whole reason."

"Look, I didn't come here to argue. I just wanted to thank you for helping my guests."

Maggie let out a heavy breath and steeled her heart. "In that case, you're welcome. Anything else I can help you with? If not, I need to start gathering my things together since I'll be leaving along with the rest of the guests in the morning," she finished in resignation.

"I said what I came here to say."

"I guess it's settled then."

****

Drake put all of his physical strength into splitting a large chunk of firewood into smaller pieces, hoping it would take some of the mental chaos from his mind. It didn't work. Maggie kept a tight hold on his thoughts no matter how he tried to stop it.

She had kept quiet during breakfast, again at lunch and now as she sat on the dock looking out at the lake. She had been there for hours, just sitting. Alone.

He slammed the sledge hammer down again, listening to the wood as it splintered and groaned beneath the torture. With three more assaults, it finally gave way and broke in two. He set the sledge hammer down and retrieved the axe to work on the smaller logs.

Glancing at the dock again, he wondered just how long the woman intended to sit there.

The rest of the guests had been quiet. Dillon and Cyndi had gone hiking, Annie and Larry stayed in their cabin, and Stephen and Beverly had taken a picnic up to a meadow he had told them about. Even Aunt Cammie had made herself scarce.

He checked his watch, noting that the afternoon had dwindled away. He set the axe down and gathered wood for the last campfire his guests would have here before leaving in the morning.

He stood, dusted off his hands and watched Maggie sit idly by the lake. Enough was enough. No one needed to sit that long on a dock, alone. He gave in to his urge and took long strides toward the dock, closing in on her fast.

He came up beside her and asked, "What do you think you're doing?"

"Excuse me?"

"You've been out here long enough. Are you trying to guilt me into saying something I don't believe?"

"Guilt you into something? No. I don't play games, Drake."

"Then why have you been sitting here all afternoon?"

"I've been praying."

That statement knocked the fight out of him. "You have?"

"Yes."

He shifted from one foot to the other. "May I sit with you?"

She nodded and looked down, fiddling with her short fingernails. "I've been trying to figure out what to expect in the future."

"And?"

"He won't tell me."

"No. I guess not." Drake chuckled, settling into the seat next to her.

"So, I have to go forward in faith."

"That's what it's all about isn't it?"

Maggie nodded. The two of them sat side by side on the dock for several more minutes without speaking. Drake tried to convince himself he was doing the right thing by sending her on her way. He knew she would stay if he spoke three simple words. But, his doubts prevented him from telling her what she needed to hear.

Drake took a deep breath, steeled his resolve and tried to think of something neutral he could talk to her about.

"Do you want to help me finish preparing for the last campfire tonight? I need to have enough wood ready for it to burn for several hours before we cook the mountain pies in it."

"Mountain pies?" She lifted her brows.

"Yeah, they cook better down in the coals."

"What is a mountain pie?"

Drake stood and reached for her hand to lift her. "You'll see. I'll make one for you tonight."

He led her to the wood pile. "Do you want to work on the kindling while I split the larger logs?"

Maggie nodded and picked up the small hatchet that sat at her feet. He watched as she took some small sticks and began slicing them into smaller pieces.

"I can hardly believe tonight's the last night."

"It does go by fast doesn't it?"

"Vacations always do."

Drake picked up the axe and chopped a few smaller pieces for Maggie to work with.

"I hope wherever I end up that I can find a church like the one you have here. I really felt at home there. Thanks again for taking me."

"It was my pleasure," he said and knew deep down he meant it.

By time they had enough firewood assembled at the fire-pit, Aunt Cammie rang the supper bell.

Cyndi and Dillon came out of the woods from their hike, and as if on cue, Stephen and Beverly soon followed. As the crowd gathered for supper, Maggie disappeared inside the kitchen, probably to help Aunt Cammie with the food.

Drake passed by Annie and Larry as he walked to his cabin. He wanted to take a quick shower before he ate. He nodded at the couple. "I hope you've enjoyed your stay here."

"Oh yes," Annie commented. "You won't hear any complaints from me."

Larry said, "Well, I have a complaint."

Annie looked shocked and Drake stopped walking.

"What is it?" Drake asked. He wanted all of his guests to have a pleasant stay.

"The food here is too good. I know I've gone and gained ten pounds." Larry chuckled as he rubbed his stomach.

Drake smiled and Annie swatted her husband on his arm. "Now don't go blamin' Aunt Cammie for that. You know you control what you put into your mouth mister."

"It's not Aunt Cammie. It's the pies and cobblers and muffins Maggie made. They're all just too good to pass up."

Drake said, "I have to agree with you." An ache settled into his gut when he realized he wouldn't be tasting anymore of her delicious treats.

"Let's go dear." Annie took her husband's arm. "We don't want to be late for supper."

"I'll see you in a few minutes." Drake waved and continued to his cabin.

****

Maggie nibbled at her food, trying to appear as happy and relaxed as the other guests seemed to be.

She watched the others carry on a conversation and realized she would miss them. She hadn't gotten to know Annie and Larry very well, but she knew enough about them to like them. Cyndi and Dillon had grown on her and she silently prayed they'd have a long and fulfilling life together.

Stephen and Beverly had made tremendous progress in their relationship. She thanked God for that, knowing he had led her to say the right things to them at the right time. Maggie watched Beverly hand a napkin to her husband. Stephen smiled at her. The scowls that had been on their faces had been replaced with something that resembled respect.

"I hope I'm not too late," Drake said as he approached the picnic table. He walked past Maggie, bringing with him the spicy scent she had learned to recognize as his.

He sat across the table from her, looking freshly shaven and smelling so good. Maggie tried not to pay attention, but found it impossible to block his commanding presence out.

"Maggie and I prepared the fire tonight for our mountain pies."

Larry said, "Here we go again." He smiled and rubbed his stomach.

Drake said, "This time it's my specialty, not Maggie's."

Maggie swallowed her bite of food as she shook her head. She reached for her napkin, patted her lips and asked, "Am I the only one here that doesn't know what a mountain pie is?"

Cyndi said, "Well, if it's what I think it is...you need a sandwich cooker, two pieces of bread, butter and apple or cherry pie filling."

"That's it," Drake answered.

Intrigued, Maggie lifted her eyebrows in question.

Drake smiled. "You'll see."

"You keep saying that."

"I keep meaning it. Tonight, it's my turn to take care of you."

Maggie warmed at his statement. Their eyes locked, and she had to concentrate on breathing as she watched tiny creases appear at the edges of his sparkling eyes when he smiled.

She nodded. "Sounds good to me."

When the sun sank behind the trees and darkness began to fall, Drake lit the fire and everyone gathered around it.

Aunt Cammie brought out warm tea and coffee before excusing herself for the night.

"Night Aunt Cammie," Maggie said. "Thanks for supper and the coffee."

"No problem, dear. It's my pleasure."

Maggie listened to the buzz of the conversation around her as the night wore on. Drake entertained the guests with stories of his past experiences in the mountains and with a few of his military deployment escapades. She couldn't help but fall deeper in love with him. The more he talked about himself the more she wanted to know. What were his days in the military like? He had mentioned sleeping in the jungle and she wondered how difficult that had been.

There was still so much she didn't know about him, and she longed to know everything. Knowing she would never get the chance kept her in a somber and quiet mood while the others continued chatting.

At one point, she noticed the conversation had dulled as Drake watched her from across the campfire. When their eyes met, he said, "I think it's time for the mountain pies."

A low murmur of agreement went through the guests and he left to go into the kitchen. A few minutes later, he came out with an iron sandwich cooker, bread, butter and pie filling. When Maggie moved to help him, he motioned for her to stay seated.

"It's my turn," he said simply and began buttering slices of bread. He put cherry pie filling on the top of one slice of bread, then closed the sandwich with a top buttered slice.

Maggie watched as he warmed the cooker in the fire and placed a sandwich inside it. He looked adept and well accustomed to cooking over a campfire, and she was drawn in, watching his practiced movements.

She observed, "It's like a grilled cheese sandwich."

"Kinda. But without the cheese. And nothing you've ever tasted compares to a sandwich cooked over the burning hot coals of a campfire."

"I don't know. The hot dogs we cooked over the fire will be hard to beat," Maggie argued.

"You can judge for yourself soon."

She nodded and said, "I can't wait."

He flashed a warm smile at her as he stood, taking the first pie out of the fire. He dumped it onto a plate and handed it to Maggie.

From the corner of her eye, she caught Cyndi wink at her and silently mouth, "Major eye-candy."

Maggie broke out into laughter and barely kept the mountain pie from falling to the ground. After it cooled, she took a bite. Drake had been right. This was even better than the hot dogs.

"Mmm. This is delicious."

Drake looked at her with amusement teasing his lips. "So you agree with me?"

"I do." She shamelessly admitted, "You were right."

Annie spoke up, "Stop dilly dallying son, I want one too."

A chorus of 'me too' rang out across the circle of guests.

"Coming right up," he promised and popped another sandwich into the cooker.

An hour later, everyone had finished their desserts and the conversation became sparse between the contented guests. Drake added two more logs to the flames before sitting down and relaxing with the rest of the group again. Maggie's eyes trailed to him as if they had a will of their own.

****

Their eyes locked over the campfire. The wind caught a tendril of Maggie's hair, blowing it into her eyes. Drake wanted to walk to her, to reach out and brush it aside.

Dillon's voice cut through his thoughts. "Is there any place close by that I could take Cyndi to see the stars? I want to do something really special on our last night here, and I thought a romantic evening under the stars would be perfect."

Drake drew his eyes from Maggie and said, "Yes. There's a fairly short hike that leads to an outcropping of boulders. If you climb the trail that begins over there," Drake pointed across the lake, "you can't miss it. Be sure to stay on the lower boulder, you can see just as well from there and it's much safer."

"Great. I owe you man."

"No problem," he said and let his eyes drift back to Maggie. She had turned her attention to Cyndi, who had started to chatter excitedly.

Drake ran a hand through his hair, wishing he could do something special for Maggie too. When she stretched and yawned, he scooted closer to the edge of his chair. She would be heading back to her cabin soon. He didn't want her to leave. Not tonight. Not tomorrow. Not ever.

He washed down the bittersweet taste in his throat with the last swallow of soda, stood and walked around the campfire to her.

Holding out his hand he said, "Come with me." He knew he wanted to be alone with her one more time.

When her lips parted in surprise and her eyebrows rose in question, he simply took her hand and led her away into the darkness.

The guest's conversations dulled as he led Maggie farther from the fire and the sounds of the forest came alive. He led her to her cabin and up onto the porch.

"Sit with me."

He heard a tremor in her voice when she

answered, "Okay."

He released her hand as they each took a seat in a rocker. He held the arms of the chair in a viselike grasp, if for no other reason than to keep himself from reaching out to her.

"Where you will go?" He asked the question that had been on his mind all day.

She hugged her arms around herself and shivered. "I don't know." She took a deep breath and exhaled slowly. "I came here to hide from Nathan and to sort out the shattered mess my life had become. I thought I could figure out how to put the pieces back together again, and plan my next move."

"Have you?"

"I've learned so much by being here with you Drake. But I still haven't figured out what to do next. Every time I think about where I want to go..." she let her words falter as she shook her head.

"Go on."

"I can't think of anywhere I'd rather be than here."

"We've been over this before."

"Yes we have. No need to tell me again how I don't fit into your world." She curled her feet up under her and asked, "So I better prepare for the unknown right? Now that I have my confidence back, how do I keep it? It seems like it would be easy to run into a problem and have a major setback."

"Remember where your confidence comes from. It comes from knowing deep down in your heart you're doing God's will. Then you know without a doubt, and no matter what anyone in the whole world says, you have the capability to do what you're supposed to do. There isn't any other way to get a stronger, more reliable confidence in yourself than to trust God's leading."

"I can feel the truth in what you say, Drake."

He turned in his chair to face her. "You can still expect bumps and ruts along the way, but if you're following His guidance, you'll make it down the right path with your confidence intact."

Maggie stood and walked to the railing. The moonlight showed the confusion in her features as she asked, "What if He's leading me to stay here?"

Drake came to stand beside her. He breathed in her cinnamon scent, trying to capture it for his memories. "I just don't see how it can work. You're a…"

"City girl. I know," Maggie interjected as she turned to face him. "I remember you telling me, at the waterfall, that you felt God calling you to a different life while you still lived in the city. You felt Him calling you to the mountains. Yet, you couldn't see a way to move at the time. Then He opened the door for you. All I'm asking is that you consider that maybe He's opening a door for us now."

Drake hadn't thought of that possibility before. Hope began to peek through his resignation, but it quickly disappeared when he remembered how long and hard he had hoped for Kara to come with him.

The silence between them stretched into minutes before Maggie pointed out, "When Stephen told Beverly he loved her, it changed their whole relationship."

"I'm still amazed by that."

"I am too. It's incredible how three simple words can mean so much and be so life changing."

"I love you…" Drake began to say and hesitated before continuing, "are three very powerful words."

He heard a tremble in her voice when she said, "They are powerful words. But they aren't the only three words that have the ability to change futures."

"I know what you want me to say Maggie. But I can't."

"I could be happy here. I am happy here."

Drake looked her over and said in a low voice, "You dropped your whole lifestyle for Nathan. You did what he wanted you to do. How do I know you aren't doing the same with me?"

He heard the pain in her voice as she asked, "How could you think that? Listen, you're not the only one who learns from mistakes. I've learned too. I would never give up who I am again to please someone else. Not even you."

"You can say that Maggie. But how can I know it for sure?"

"You're a man of faith. How about putting a little bit of your faith in me?"

Chapter Twenty

In the morning, Maggie packed her suitcases slowly, drawing out the little time she had left at the resort. Drake hadn't said the three words she'd been hoping for last night. She tried to accept his decision, she had to.

She hadn't felt this torn about leaving somewhere since she left her parents to attend college so many years ago. Even then, it hadn't been as difficult as this. *Drake may have a little to do with it.* She smiled at her thoughts, knowing he had everything to do with it.

When she snapped her suitcases shut, her hope snapped shut with them. She took a deep breath and looked around the cabin, checking drawers and cabinets for any remaining belongings. She checked under the bed and let out a small laugh, remembering when she had first arrived and checked under it for dust bunnies. Finally convinced she had all of her things, she took one last, long look at the cabin before dragging her suitcases outside.

Harley's Piper came skimming the tops of the trees as she made her way down the path. She saw Beverly and Stephen on their porch, rocking side by side.

Beverly stood and came to the railing as Maggie passed by their cabin. "Hey, Maggie. I wanted to thank you for all you've done for us." She glanced back at her husband and smiled.

"You're welcome. I'm glad you've worked things out."

"We're still working through some things," Stephen said and stood. "So, we've decided to stay on another two weeks here. This time we can concentrate more on making up with each other, rather than fighting with each other." He wrapped an arm around Beverly's waist and kissed her cheek.

Beverly blushed, looked at Maggie and said, "Thanks again. Goodbye."

Maggie nodded. "Take care of each other." She walked the rest of the way to the picnic table, and Cyndi and Dillon came out of the kitchen.

Cyndi said, "I wish we had more time here."

"So do I," Maggie agreed.

Cyndi surprised her with a big hug and Dillon nodded and said, "It's nice to have met you."

"You too."

Dillon said, "You were the last fly out here Maggie. You shouldn't have to wait for all of us again. Why don't you fly back first? Annie and Larry aren't even up yet."

"Thanks Dillon, but I'm not in a hurry. I wanted to say bye to Aunt Cammie first."

Cyndi said, "Oh, she's still asleep. It's only seven-thirty and we didn't want to wake her, so we helped ourselves to an early breakfast."

Dillon admitted, "We were hoping to get one last hike in this morning…"

Maggie nodded. "I can fly back first then. It's not a problem."

Cyndi grinned. "Thanks Maggie. Take care. Come on Dillon, let's go." Cyndi took her husband's hand and they hurried away.

She sensed Drake behind her before he even spoke a word or made a sound. Without turning around she said, "I'm glad you didn't turn out to be a bear."

Drake let out a deep rumble of laughter and asked, "Are you sure about that? I acted like one on more than one occasion didn't I?"

She pasted a smile on her face and turned to face him. "I deserved it…most of the time anyway."

He reached out and handed her a cup of coffee, then he threw a hand in the air and waved at Harley who busied himself tinkering with the seaplane.

Drake said, "I'm driving into town after I get the cabins cleaned out for the next guests. I could take you with me if you'd rather not fly."

Maggie glanced at the seaplane. "It doesn't scare me as much as it did before. I'll be okay."

He nodded his head and studied his coffee for a moment. He looked up and started to speak in a low voice, "Maggie I never wanted to hurt you..."

"I know you didn't. Listen, I think it's better if I just go now." She set the remainder of her coffee on the picnic table and reached for her luggage.

Drake immediately set his coffee down and took her suitcases out of her grasp saying, "I'll get them for you."

Maggie nodded and headed down the dock. She walked carefully as she remembered what it felt like to fall into the cold lake water. A chill went through her at the memories, and she stayed clear of the edges.

Harley climbed in first and Drake loaded the luggage. When he finished, Maggie gave him a brief hug and said, "Goodbye Drake." She scurried into the plane, praying she could hold back the tears until he could no longer see her.

She felt him watching her as she settled into her seat. She tugged on her bottom lip, took in a breath then turned to face him. His jaw clenched and his brows drew together as he reached for the door and shut it between them.

Maggie kept her eyes locked with his through the window. *Accept me.* She pleaded with him through her eyes and pressed her palm to the window. Stark pain erupted on his hardened features. He swallowed, then turned and walked away with her heart, leaving Maggie with an emptiness inside that rivaled none she had ever known.

Tears fell swift and silent from her eyes as Harley started the seaplane's engine. He checked the gauges before looking at her. "Are you sure you're ready?"

Maggie nodded.

Harley tipped his head. "It sucks going back to reality doesn't it?"

"I think I got a pretty good dose of reality right here Harley."

"I guess so," he said looking at the tears on her cheeks.

"I'm okay. We should go."

"Do you think you'll need the bag?"

She smiled through her tears. "I think I'll be okay this time. But thanks anyway."

Maggie closed her eyes as the plane taxied along the water, trying to ward off the pain of leaving her heart behind.

****

"I can't believe you let her go," Aunt Cammie said coming to stand in the cabin's doorway.

"Better now than later isn't it?" Drake asked as he pulled the sheets from the bed. He kept his focus on his task and didn't stop to look his aunt in the eye. He knew what he would find on her face, and he didn't want to deal with her disapproval at the moment.

"What makes you so sure she'd leave later on anyway?" Aunt Cammie paused, took a breath and added, "I've never known you to give up on someone before even giving them a chance."

"I can't make her into what she isn't." He gathered the used sheets and placed them into a laundry basket.

"And what is she Drake?"

He stood tall, grabbed a clean set of sheets and said, "She's from the city."

"Yeah? Well son, in case you forgot...so are you.

Does that mean you're going to eventually leave here too?"

Drake ignored her question and began making up the bed. Aunt Cammie remained silent until he had finished tucking in the comforter and adding chocolates on top of the pillows. He finally looked at her and saw concern in her eyes where he thought he would only see disapproval.

"I have one more question for you before I head into town," Aunt Cammie said as she pulled a set of keys out of her purse and jangled them between her fingers.

"What's that?"

"What traits would a woman need to have to be able to be happy here with you?"

"That's easy." He sat on the edge of the bed. "To begin with, she would have to like it here. To like being outside. She would have to be courageous. Courteous and kind to the guests. She'd have to be someone who didn't need to be entertained all the time. Someone who could be content to sit at the campfire every night. Someone who would be satisfied reading a book on the rainy days. She'd have face challenges without backing down. She'd have to be a woman who could stand on her own..." Drake's voice faded as his heart jammed in his chest and his jaw hardened. He took a sharp breath and asked, "I just described Maggie didn't I?"

Aunt Cammie nodded solemnly, turned and walked away, leaving him alone with his thoughts.

Maggie was all those things he had just described, and more. The answer lay heavily on his shoulders and twisted him in the gut. He ground his teeth together and stepped outside, looking toward the sky in the direction the seaplane had carried her as if he could bring her back with his will.

She had told him she felt like God wanted her here. While Drake had followed his leading to come to the wilderness, he had ignored what Maggie had considered as her leading, even after he had encouraged her to follow God's guidance.

He hadn't trusted God to open the doors for him to move to the wilderness and now he hadn't trusted God to lead the right woman to him. But He had, and Drake had pushed her away out of fear. He felt regret and a touch of shame wash over him as he realized he had made the same mistake in not trusting God again.

He ran a hand through his hair, as a new fear erupted inside him. *Am I too late?*

He dropped into a rocker on the porch and placed his hands on his face. The enormity of his decision played over in his mind as he began to pray. *Lord, I thank you for who you are and I thank you for loving me. Thank you for bringing Maggie here. I don't know what your will is for our lives, but I pray that it is done, because I know your plan is way better than anything I could ever imagine. Please forgive me for not trusting you again, and forgive me for sending her away. Please keep the door open a little bit longer and guide me in what to do. Thank you Lord. Amen.*

Chapter Twenty-One

Maggie drifted along the quaint village stores, idly looking at the various trinkets and touristy items. She briefly considered buying a postcard of the mountains, but decided it would be too much of a reminder of what she had left behind.

She had loaded her suitcases in her car as soon as she arrived, but couldn't bring herself to put the key in the ignition and drive away. So, she procrastinated in the shops, telling herself it was because she had nowhere she had to be. But deep inside she knew she just didn't want to leave.

She came up to Jenkins store and smiled ironically, remembering how Drake had looked at Jenkins and claimed her as his for two weeks. She had no idea how true that would turn out to be. She entered the shop and found Jenkins standing behind the counter. She waited for him to finish ringing up a customer before walking over to him.

"Hi. Remember me?" she asked with a smile.

"Now how could I ever forget such a lovely lady? How was your time at Drake's Retreat?"

Maggie didn't quite know how to answer him so she said simply, "Better than I had ever expected."

He nodded and smiled back at her. "That's good to hear. Aunt Cammie told me you had some adventures along the way. Did you really climb up that mountain on your own?"

"Yes, but don't remind me. Drake came after me, and let me tell you, he wasn't too happy about it."

Jenkins grinned. "He told me you were going to be trouble."

"He did?"

"Yep. I guess he was right." He gave her a wink.

"I guess so. Hey, you said Aunt Cammie told you about my mountain escapade. When did she tell you?"

"A few minutes ago. She's in the back there." He indicated a door at the back of the store. "I let her use the office space on occasion. Right now, she's interviewing for an assistant in her kitchen."

Maggie's heart sped up. "I was hoping to say goodbye to her. I missed her this morning."

"Go on back and wait at the door. She should be finishing up soon."

"Thanks." Maggie walked to the back of the store. She didn't have to wait long before the door opened and a small, older woman scooted out. Maggie spotted Aunt Cammie sitting behind a desk, running a hand through her hair and looking weary.

"Hi," Maggie said tentatively. "I just came by to say..."

"You're hired."

"W-wait I just..."

"I declare, I was beginning to think I'd be on my own forever. You should have seen some of the people who thought they could handle this job," Aunt Cammie said as if she hadn't heard her words. Then her face brightened and she stood, came around the desk and hugged Maggie tightly. "I'm so glad you're here."

"I didn't know Drake had agreed to get a new assistant for you."

"I have you to thank for that. He said you talked to him about it and convinced him it was time. And now here you come wandering right in to the interviews. You're the perfect fit for the job."

"Aunt Cammie I can't...Drake..."

"Posh. You can and you will. I need you, honey. I can't keep going like I have been. Please help me out here."

"I-I don't know." Despite Maggie's trepidation,

the thought about going back sent a thrill of excitement through her, and she knew Aunt Cammie really did need the help. She took a bite of her lower lip.

"You're more than qualified…"

"That's not what I mean. Drake doesn't…"

"I'll tell you what Drake doesn't. He doesn't know what's good for him. But I do. Come on. I'll take you home."

"He sent me away."

"Well I'm bringing you back."

"He won't want me there."

"Hogwash."

Maggie tilted her head and couldn't help but to laugh.

"It's my decision who to hire, and I'm choosing you. If he doesn't like it…then too bad."

"I don't know. I just…"

"Come on. Out the door with you." Aunt Cammie began ushering her out the door. She waved at Jenkins. "This girl's too good to let go. I've decided I'm keeping her."

He smiled. "I don't blame you." Then he addressed Maggie. "There's no use fighting her. Once she has her mind made up, you might as well give in."

Aunt Cammie grinned. "That's true. Let's get your car and head on back. We've got a full crew coming in this afternoon." She shuffled Maggie out the door. "Now, which car is yours?"

She pointed to a compact car at the far end of the lot. "But where will I stay?"

"I've got a spare bedroom that will be perfect for you. Now stop worrying." When Aunt Cammie saw her car, she shook her head. "That won't do. That little thing wouldn't make it past Smugglers Pass. It gets real steep on that section of the road. I tell you what, you get your bags and ride with me. We can worry about what to do with your car later."

"But…"

"No buts. Come on now, I'll help you with your luggage."

Maggie discovered Jenkins had been right. There was no changing Aunt Cammie's mind once she made it up.

By time they arrived back at the resort, Maggie had chewed her lip into soreness with worry.

"Aunt Cammie, what if Drake really doesn't want me to come back?"

"I'll tell you what dear. Let's consider this a trial period. If it doesn't work out after these two weeks are up, you can go on your way. Deal?"

Maggie relented. "Deal." But she still carried a great amount of anxiety with her as Aunt Cammie backed the SUV up to the kitchen door.

"I've got supplies in the back there. You can start your new job right now and help me unload 'em."

"Sure," Maggie agreed and added, "You know, I'd help you for free."

"I know dear. I know." Aunt Cammie patted her hand and climbed out.

****

Maggie's respect for Aunt Cammie grew exponentially as the day wore on. After unloading the supplies and re-stocking the pantry and refrigerator, they washed loads of sheets and towels in between making preparations for dinner.

"I don't know how you've been doing all of this by yourself," Maggie commented.

"It's been hard. Drake does more than his fair share, but it has still been rough at times. Honestly, the switch-over days are the hardest."

"Switch-over?"

"Yeah," Aunt Cammie said as she washed lettuce in the sink. "Switching from one set of guests to the other. Sometimes Drake gives us a day or two lapse between guests. That makes it easier. Would you be a dear and make something for dessert?"

"Sure. You've got everything I need for several weeks worth of desserts."

"You mean *we've* got everything you need."

Maggie smiled. "You're always trying to make me feel at home."

"Well, you are home now, dear."

"That'll be up to Drake to decide won't it?"

"He let me make the decision of who to hire..."

"I know, but I need to be honest with you. I'll only stay if Drake agrees."

Aunt Cammie nodded and brushed a little flour from Maggie's shoulder. "I have a feeling that won't be a problem."

She wondered what Aunt Cammie meant as she reached for the sugar.

"After you finish up dessert, I want you to take the rest of the night getting settled in. Make yourself at home in the spare bedroom. What's mine is yours."

"But what about dinner?"

"You've already helped me enough today, dear." When Maggie started to protest, Aunt Cammie said, "I'll tell you what. You take the night off and get up early, make those sinfully delicious cinnamon buns of yours for breakfast and we'll call it even."

Maggie knew better than to argue with her. "Okay. It's a deal."

The next morning, Maggie woke up extra early to begin making the buns. She had stayed in her new room the night before and hadn't seen Drake yet. She kept telling herself she wasn't hiding from him, but deep down she knew she had been delaying seeing him. She couldn't bare it if he sent her packing again. Despite what Aunt Cammie thought, Maggie had a feeling she'd be moving on in another two weeks.

Maggie picked up a tray of hot cinnamon buns and headed toward the door with her stomach churning and her heart hammering in her chest she prayed, *Please, Lord, help me to face Drake and stand firm if he rejects my presence here, again.*

She swallowed down her trepidation as she pushed open the door, letting it slam shut behind her. She immediately did a sweep of the resort looking for Drake, but didn't see him anywhere. She saw Beverly and Stephen at the table, instantly relieved at the sight of the two familiar faces. Two other couples sat at the table, and as she approached, they each greeted her and told her their names.

At least this time she only had to remember four new names instead of six. She smiled at the new guests, and their names when right out of her head. She thought, *Oh well. Here I go again.*

She headed back to the kitchen and passed Aunt Cammie on her way out. "How do you remember everyone's names?"

Aunt Cammie chuckled. "I have a copy of the guest list. I know the names beforehand, and all I have to do is match the names to the faces, then I'm set."

"So that's the secret. I'll have to check out that list next time." *If there is a next time,* she reminded herself.

Maggie kept busy cleaning the kitchen for the next several minutes. She tried to keep calm, but failed miserably. He hands shook nervously as she wiped the counter raw with a dishcloth.

She jumped when Drake came slamming through the door in a sprint. His eyes immediately locked with hers. He held a cinnamon bun in his hand, the icing dripping from his fingers.

He smiled, releasing his gorgeous dimple and said, "I recognized your buns the moment I saw them."

Maggie's pulse leapt and her face heated. His smile encouraged her to ask, "Should I assume they still impress you?"

"Have no doubt about that." He grinned and set the bun on the counter. He licked the remaining icing from his fingers as he stepped around the counter to join her.

"I wasn't sure how you'd feel about Aunt Cammie hiring me. If you don't want me here..." hesitancy marked her words.

Drake closed the remaining distance between them and without hesitating wrapped his arms around her and devoured her lips with his. Moments later, breathless, he broke apart from her and whispered, "I want you here, Maggie." He lifted her chin with his thumb and added, "I should have never let you go. I was afraid it was too late." His eyes searched hers.

"You want me here?" She could hardly believe what he had just said and that he had just kissed her.

"I do."

"But you were so adamant..."

"I was wrong."

"What happened to change your mind?"

Drake explained, "Aunt Cammie asked me to describe the type of woman that could be happy living out here."

"And?"

"And I described you."

Maggie's hope flickered to life again. She dared to believe, but she still needed to know. "If you really want me here...if you really want me to stay...I need to hear you say it. Say the three words I've been waiting for."

Drake looked deep into her soul and answered, "You belong here."

Tears erupted from Maggie's eyes. She let them flow down her cheeks without reserve, without shame. She lifted her hands, placed them on his face and said, "Those are three very powerful words."

"Words that have the potential to change lives?"

Maggie nodded and smiled. "Absolutely."

"Then you'll stay?"

She nodded. "There's no other place I'd rather be."

"I believe you." Drake's smile widened. "And I love you, Maggie."

Her heart leapt in anticipation. She laughed through her tears. "Does this mean we finally have a truce, Mr. Strong?"

"I'll make you a deal." He stood back and held out his hand, inviting her to shake it. When she placed her hand in his he said, "We'll have a truce if you'll agree to be my wife."

Maggie's knees felt weak. She watched Drake kneel before her as the handshake turned into a caress.

She said without hesitation, "Then we have a truce, Mr. Strong."

Maggie's broad, lumberjack of a man stared at her in silence, once again. This time his eyes roamed over her, they were filled with love.

She melted to the floor and into his embrace. "Does this mean I can travel up the mountain on my own now?"

He shook his head. "No, baby. It means you don't have to." His lips met hers with a quiet urgency that filled every remaining need inside her.

Aunt Cammie burst into the kitchen. "We need more muffins and buns, Maggie. The new crowd's eatin' them up faster than I can take them out." She stopped in her tracks as she spotted Maggie and Drake sitting on the floor. "Good heavens, are you hurt?"

Maggie and Drake laughed in unison and Drake spoke up, "No one's hurt. In fact, we couldn't be any better."

"Drake just proposed to me." Maggie knew the priceless look Aunt Cammie gave her would remain imprinted on her heart forever.

Aunt Cammie clasped her hands together and did a jig right there in the middle of the kitchen floor. "My Drake's getting married!" She fanned her face and said, "I declare, we'd better get to planning your wedding. We've got less than two weeks…"

"Two weeks?" Drake and Maggie each asked at the same time.

"Yeah. Didn't you know? One of our new guests is a pastor."

Maggie set her questioning eyes on Drake. "I guess it's meant to be. What do you think?"

"I think the two weeks can't get here fast enough," Drake replied and swept her into his loving embrace.

About the Author...

"I've been hooked on reading romance novels ever since I picked one up over twenty years ago. That's also when my own imagination started to roll, and it hasn't stopped since. When I finally realized that it was God who put it into my heart to write, I knew my dreams of becoming an author could turn into a reality. I am a member of the Romance Writers of America and continue to be an avid reader. When not writing, I spend my energy chasing around my beautiful young children, enjoying my own real-life hero, and watching movies with friends."

Visit Wendy at www.wendydavy.com

Printed in the United States
132883LV00001B/127-165/P

9 781601 543288